The WAR for the LOT

The
WAR for
the LOT

A Tale of Fantasy and Terror

Sterling E. Lanier

Illustrations by Robert Baumgartner

FOLLETT PUBLISHING COMPANY
Chicago   New York

SBN 695-49168-7   Titan edition
SBN 695-89168-5   Trade edition

Library of Congress Catalog Card Number: 69-10262

First Printing

I

To my beloved wife —
critic, editor, typist
and muse

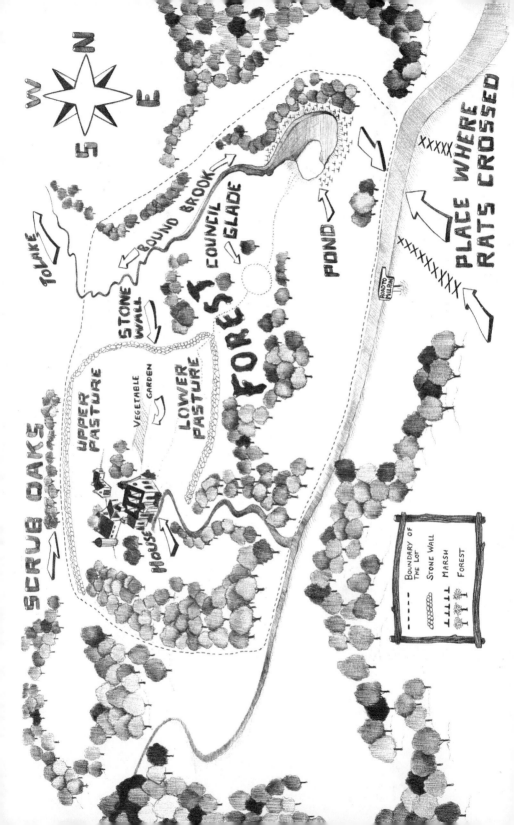

Prologue

Silence lay upon the woodland called The Lot. The spring starlight, filtering through the silver birches and oaks, touched the dark laurels beneath but only increased the blackness below them. Along the old stone wall, the poison ivy clung in thick clumps, mixed with strands of honeysuckle and wild grape.

Shadows drifted from the top of a tall tulip tree to the trunk of a lofty beech, only the scratch of tiny claws on bark and the windless night betraying the flying squirrels, revealing them as alive and not the last of the winter leaves drifting down in the soft air.

A few hardy crickets had begun to sing, foreshadowing the full-blown insect chorus of the high summer. But the main body of the night's music came from the pond and bog at the north end of the wood, where frogs were finishing their annual spring song among the reeds and wild flags.

Deeper in the wood, along Bound Brook, the scrub willows grew in patches, providing cover for the Jack-in-the-pulpits on their tall stems, the wide leaves of skunk cabbage, and the drooping fronds of fern.

The flavor of green and growing things perfumed the New England night, and the peaceful wood seemed to dream of the summer cycle of warmth and upwelling, of increase and birth, oft-repeated and always new.

Yet, to an observer wise in the ways of the forest, something would seem different, odd perhaps. Under the countless scurryings on the floor of the wood, the tiny movements of shrews and the mousefolk in the leafmold, there was urgency of a new and frightening kind. The small bickerings of the chipmunks along the old wall were taut with something besides the usual feeding, play, and nest-building. From a boulder in Bound Brook, old Scratch, the big raccoon, was fishing for freshwater mussels, his clever hands dabbling in the white sand, yet with his whole body strained and tense. Even the frog music from the swamp seemed to vibrate on a note of strangeness and fear.

Fear. That was the clue. Throughout the whole wood, and out into the starlit pastures beyond, from one end of The Lot to the other, there ran a current, subtler but more pervasive than electricity. From the smallest birds huddled on their night perches down to the newest muskrat kit in its house deep in the bog, the same thrill sent a warning.

The Lot was afraid.

1

Through the window next to his bed, the brown eyes of Alexander Geoffrey March sleepily surveyed the sky of late evening. He was very tired, but still so excited about his day that he had to think about it some more. At his age, new experiences crowded in so quickly that there was hardly time to even have them, let alone think about them properly. And what an incredible day!

The night before, Alec had said good-bye to his mother and father for the entire summer. His parents had also been upset, but they knew that the boy's grandfather would look after him properly. Old Professor March, until his retirement to the Connecticut countryside, had been one of the leading medieval historians in the world. A healthy, tough old man, long a widower, he had been only too happy to have his young grandson for the summer. His housekeeper, Mrs. Darden, and her husband, John, who had looked after Professor March for many years, were equally pleased.

Alec's father, a marine designer, had been offered a contract which would require him to live for three months in the Far East. His wife would accompany him. It meant living in hotels and moving constantly about from one country to another as Mr. March examined shipyards, saw foreign dignitaries, and dealt with fellow engineers from other countries. The offer from Professor March to take Alec for the summer on his old farm, The Lot, seemed a godsend.

The Dardens were childless, but Louisa Darden, a thin lath of a woman with warm blue eyes, had long been known as the finest nurse in the whole area of Mill Run, Connecticut. She was a member of a family which had first settled Mill Run in the seventeenth century and never allowed John Darden, a "foreigner" from New Milford, forty whole miles away, to forget it.

John was a tall, silent man in his sixties, who kept the house and its surrounding lawn and garden in wonderful order. He was one of the last of a vanishing race, the New Englander who could do anything. No machine, from the power mower to a delicate French clock on the study mantle, was too intricate for him to fix. His large vegetable garden produced asparagus and strawberries no hothouse could have bettered. He was a wonderful shot, and crows and woodchucks gave both his vegetable garden and his flower beds a wide berth. But John never hunted for sport and the wild things had learned many years ago that they could do what they liked as long as the vegetables and flowers were left alone.

Both John and the Professor were agreed in refusing to allow hunters or trappers into The Lot at any season of the year, and its acres were a sanctuary for animals and birds. In the deer-hunting season, the beautiful creatures cropped the lawn within full view of the house. During a hard winter, piles of hay would appear mysteriously in the upper pastures along with blocks of pink rock salt. John never mentioned these unless questioned, and then would only mutter something about not wanting "to have the bark eaten off the fruit trees by a lot of worthless varmints."

The great apple and pear trees, in appearance at least dating back to the original settlers, grew all about the house, although not encroaching on the lawn. Several clumps of them grew even in the pastures. They were always carefully pruned, although they produced more fruit than ten families could have eaten in a year. *Somebody* ate the fruit, however, and a stroller walking out on a late summer evening under the trees could hear the rush of small feet as the night's diners fled.

Birds abounded on The Lot. Quail loved the overgrown pastures and cock pheasants called under the very windows of the house. The drummings of a male ruffed grouse echoed from the depths of the wood, and at intervals in the evening the strange and lovely song of a courting woodcock spiraled down from the sky over the lower swamp.

Baltimore orioles hung their basket nests from the two giant elms which shaded the front walk, and house wrens disputed nesting sites on the roof of the wide porch and under the eaves. Robins haunted the lawn and the garden, and blue jays flashed from the wood to the orchard and back, pursued by smaller birds whose nests they had robbed. Bird song encompassed the house during the summer days and the calls of whippoorwills and owls rang from the shadowed trees at night.

Alec had visited the old house with his parents on two or three occasions previously, but had never been there for longer than a weekend, and that in winter. A city boy, his first day in early June had seemed an endless round of new and interesting sights.

He had followed John on his rounds of work and had been presented with an oak-handled spade of his own—"so you can help me feed the house," John said.

Carrying this acquisition, Alec had next made the acquaintance of the house tomcat, a stout, lazy, orange fellow named Worthless—" 'cause he is. I seen mice running over him while he lay there wide awake!"—who followed them about, a bell on his collar jingling softly. The bell had been placed there so that even a very careless bird could get out of Worthless' way.

John had made Alec listen until he heard the

clear song of the white-throated sparrow.

"That's a Peabody bird. Hear him? 'Peabody, Peabody,' over and over."

Then he had been shown how to put pellets of moist cat food on a stone near the old well, until a fat, mottled brown toad had emerged and gobbled them up, much to the annoyance of Worthless, who was held firmly by the collar. The golden eyes of the toad had blinked at the boy and seemed to say something strange and wild.

Amused and pleased by this, he had next been led to a small, newly made pen near the back stairs to the kitchen. The pen held a pile of leaves, a bowl of water, some cut-up vegetables and a handsome yellow-and-black box turtle, who on spying the visitors, instantly came over and begged some of the cat food.

"Pick him up," urged John. "I found him in my garden, the varmint, digging for worms after a rain. He don't bite. There's a lot of critters around for a boy to play with. He's your first, but we'll get plenty more. Put him down now and we'll poke around a bit over the place. There's a lot to see."

Replacing his first country pet carefully on the leaves, Alec promised mentally to pay him a visit as soon as possible. A family of turtles would be fun, he thought.

John led the boy at an easy ramble around the house and up into the pasture on the hill behind it, talking in a quiet voice as he explained the layout of The Lot.

"I dunno why it's called The Lot. Actually, there's at least eight lots in the whole setup, but the whole place has been *The* Lot, Lou says, since there was nobody here 'cept Indians! She ought to know, 'cause her folks been here since then. I asked her once if her folks *was* Indians, but she took on so, I didn't push it none. She's funny about some things, for a fact.

"Anyway, look down there. That's our patch of woods, to the left of the house and reaching up the hill here towards us. That ain't the house first built here either, although it's old enough, around Civil War times. But there was two houses earlier on that site.

"Your Grandpa picked it up for a song in the 'thirties. He didn't want to farm, just fixed up the house and used the barn to put his car in. Seems a pity not to farm, but there's no living in it nowadays, not in Connecticut. When I was a boy over to New Milford, it was all farms through here and only a few factories."

John pointed with a large brown hand. "See there, where the drive comes in from the road? Now you go left and there's Mill Run village where you can just see the Congregational church steeple over the trees. Maybe you can go to church on Sundays with me and Lou, if your Grandpa don't mind.

"Our land stops over there on the right, by the

long wire fence. That's a camp for Scouts, all that forest area, and the boys come up from the city and camp there and stravagle around in the woods all summer. Does 'em good, I tell you, but I wish they wouldn't light fires so durn much, even if they have them counselors with them.

"Now, here behind us again the boundary goes to that old wall. There's a big lake a long way over there, full of city people in little shacks all round, till you can't see the water for laundry and mailboxes. They got so many outboard motors on the lake the fish don't dare move off the bottom, and I hate to think what the sewage goes into."

The easy contempt of the countryman showed in his voice, bred from generations of men and women who disliked crowding and were invincibly suspicious of cities and the value thereof.

"So you see, sonny, we're on kind of a triangle here."

The big hand traced a rough triangle in the pasture's loam, where a fox had overturned a rock in search of mice the night before.

"Up here, near the point, there's the house, on the left side. There's good second-growth woods over most of the place, but in the parts that get sun, you look out for poison ivy. After a while you'll keep away by instinct, like."

He had showed Alec the three glossy leaves on their short stem, and warned him of the way the treacherous plant could wear different colors, being red, yellow or green seemingly at whim.

"I expect you'll get it anyway, but it ain't bad on most people. Just tell Lou if you begin to itch. She knows a poultice that's better than anything the doc can do for it.

"Now down here, there's a brook we call Bound Brook. Must have been a boundary once, I guess. Goes through the woods down to Musquash Pond. I had it tested and it's over five miles of scrub oak and brush to the spring it starts from. So you can drink it. Don't tell Lou that, though; she thinks any water from outside will make you sick."

John winked one blue eye as he spoke, and Alec winked back, conscious of the trust imposed in him.

"There's little pools in the woods, where the brook widens," continued John, "just the right size for you to go swimming on hot days. I'll show you some and maybe we can dig them wider yet, for a real swim. . . . Well, that's about it for now. Let's go see what Lou has for lunch. It's around noon and I'm hungry!"

After a hearty meal, Alec had gone to look for his grandfather.

He found him working in his study, a vast, rambling room on the first floor, full of walnut bookshelves right up to the ceiling and pleasantly lit by large windows along the outside wall. Books were everywhere—on tables, in corners and even on the floor. In the middle of the room was an enormous, rolltop desk, also covered with books. In a swivel chair of an antique variety, made of fumed oak and heavily padded with dark leather, sat Professor March, a small, square, ruddy old gentleman, with a closely trimmed white mustache and a shock of coarse white hair bristling on his head.

His studies had apparently overcome him, for his head was bowed on his breast and a resonant snore proclaimed at fixed intervals that his thoughts were more than wandering.

But he awoke at once upon Alec's gentle knock on a corner of the desk, and clearing his throat, glared affectionately at his grandson.

"Well, Alexander, good to see you. I was musing over a commentary on Irenaeus—ah—lucubrating, as it were, upon the question of his alleged laxness with heresy. But it can wait, it can wait! What can I do for you?"

"I thought you were asleep," said Alec, provoking a series of "harumphs" and, "No, no, nothing of the sort's," which finally died away under the boy's stare.

"Well," said the Professor, sheepishly, "I *was* asleep. As a matter of fact, I sleep a lot. I'm seventy-two, you know, Alec, and despite what they say, old people like me do sleep a lot. We just don't do it all at once like younger people, but take little naps all the time. Sometimes, when you've been in bed for hours, I'm down here working. I mean really working, not pretending to, as I was just now. So you may find me resting from time to time. If the door's not shut, come in and wake me up. If it is, I really need peace and quiet. Now—what's on your mind?"

"John told me about how you bought the house," said Alec. "Could you tell me more about The Lot?"

The Professor looked reflective.

"It's a funny place, in some ways," he said, "but it suits me. There used to be legends about it. Lou told me some of them, as a matter of fact. There are always more animals around here than in any other part of the country, and apparently the original Indians never hunted in this particular area unless they were starving. They were a small tribe, an offshoot of the Mohegans. They served as shamans— medicine men and priests, you know—to the other Indians around here. They didn't allow hunting, even by the first white settlers, in any of this area. They were pretty rough about it until they died out or were run off.

"Lou can tell you more, but that's why John doesn't hunt and, frankly, one reason why I don't allow hunting or trapping. The Lot was the center of all the sacred territory, and the Indian priests used to hold ceremonies in the woods down there."

"When did they leave?" asked Alec.

"Long ago. The last Indians moved out in 1780 or thereabouts. Still," he continued, "you'll see lots of

18

animals around. I gather from Lou and your parents that you like animals?"

"They interest me more than anything!" said the boy. "I want to study them when I'm older, but I read all about them now. Mom lets me go to the two zoos and the American Museum of Natural History in New York, and I know some of the scientific names of mammals and birds."

"Hm," mused the Professor, cocking one eyebrow at the boy. "From medieval studies to marine engineering to zoology in three generations. Not a bad mix. . . . Now," he continued, "it's too nice a day to stay in—for *you* that is—and *I* am going to do some real work. Why don't you explore some more? Don't go too far from the house until you know the lay of the land better."

Alec promptly took this advice and set off outside, steering for the gray, tumbledown stone wall along the brow of the hill. As the sun warmed his bare head and a gentle breeze ruffled his brown hair, he watched a ragged flight of black crows drift over, cawing hoarsely at the sight of him. When they had vanished, a blue jay came and sat on a branch not ten feet away and stared, first with one bright eye, then the other, until Alec laughed at the twisting azure head and frightened the bird away. On and on he strolled, until he had passed far out of sight of the house.

He sat down finally in the shade of a large oak

and simply watched the old wall and its life, somehow realizing that he would see more when not in motion himself.

It was very hot now. He had walked for almost an hour. Insects buzzed around him and birds called in almost deafening numbers. Along the wall, he noticed the striped chipmunks darting about, although none came close to him. He watched a large brownish-gray bird, a mourning dove, eating berries and walking about on its short legs through a dense cluster of poison ivy. He decided that the bird was not affected by the plant's poison and made a mental note to ask John if this was true of all wild animals.

Alec sat down. The blend of bird and insect voices and the heat had made him drowsy. Half-asleep, he was just closing his eyes when a rustle of leaves came from the left. He saw a beautiful black-and-white animal, the size of a cat, with a long bushy tail held proudly in the air, calmly surveying him from not more than a yard away.

He watched, strangely unafraid, as the skunk sat up on its short hind legs and sniffed, peering shortsightedly at him and wrinkling its pink nose. Its small forepaws were tucked into its chest, like a squirrel's, and it rocked slightly on its haunches as it stared at him.

Another human, I see. It looks small; no doubt a cub or half grown. Harmless, I guess, no nasty smell or metal. Wonder where it came from? Oh well, I

*can't sit here all day like some I could name. Will it
throw stones? Probably. But there you are, you can't
have everything. I'll go into the trees where it can't
aim. Just one more interruption. Still, as I say, we
can't have everything.*

When Alec finally moved, the skunk had long since
departed, having climbed the broken wall and trun-
dled steadily off under the trees and into the undergrowth.

The sun had gone down quite a bit toward the brow
of the hill behind the house, when the boy, feeling
slightly cold and stiff, got up and walked slowly home.

He trudged up the gentle shoulder of the hill,
kicking the tall, new grass and weeds until he passed
under the old fruit trees and reached the edge of the
lawn by the side of the house. Here he turned to stare
back at the wood. The tall trees, radiant in the light of
late afternoon, nodded and swayed in the golden air,
green, impenetrable and silent.

Alec began to run toward the house, turning the
corner and flying to the back steps, head down and
breathless, caught up in a sudden feeling of apprehension.

Here he was brought to a sudden stop by running
smack into Lou Darden, who was coming with an arm-
load of wash which she had removed from the clothes-
line.

Barely managing to avoid falling backwards, wash
and all, she recovered her footing and stared hard at

Alec. She had seen at a glance that the boy's set white face and abstracted expression meant some kind of problem.

"Now, honey, tell Lou. Something give you a scare? A snake, maybe?" She knew that a few copperheads lived in the woods and that, rarely, a rattler moved down out of the hills from the northwest.

Alec only shook his head mutely. For a minute they stood facing one another, Lou puzzled by his reluctance to speak. Then he sat down and looked up into her wise eyes and lined face.

"Lou," he said slowly, "is there anything funny about the woods down there? Does—does anyone live there?"

The woman also sat down on the lowest step, cradling the laundry, and beckoned wordlessly to the boy to come close. For a moment they sat together in silence.

"Did you see something, boy? Or hear it?" she asked quietly.

"I thought I did," he answered. "I thought I heard an animal talk, Lou. But I know that's not possible. Is it? I just day-dreamed it, didn't I?"

For a space of seconds, the old woman stared at him. She looked away before answering.

"Some can hear them," she said finally. "My brother, Jared, could. He's been dead and gone, nigh on thirty years now, but he could do it. Not often and not always. And mark you—only around here!"

She sighed, rose and laid the wash carefully over

the back porch rail and then reseated herself on the step, smoothing out her white apron.

"I used to think I heard the birds and critters talking when I was little, younger than you. I expect most small children do. We played all over this area when we was young and school was out. But Jared was different. My family, the Griders, have been here since the white men first came to Mill Run." Her voice dropped until it was almost a whisper.

"And maybe earlier yet. It ain't nothing to brag on, but my granny told me once, when I was sassing her, that I was a throwback to Chief Paccomuc, and no wonder! I asked my ma what she meant later on and she took on something terrible, wouldn't speak about it at all, and told me I was a bad girl.

"But I asked Pa one night when she'd gone to bed, and he didn't seem so het up or surprised. He said we was supposed to have Indian blood in the family and that one of his early great-grands had married a daughter of Paccomuc, the biggest medicine chief in all Connecticut."

She smoothed her apron again and then glared sternly at Alec, whose wide, brown eyes stared blankly back.

"Now don't you go repeatin' this, not to Darden or your grandpa or *nobody,*" she went on. "It's my business who my family was, and I'm telling you for a reason. My brother Jared told me time and again never to say nothin' to anyone. We were close, me and

Jared, being only a year apart in age. He told me he was going to shoot a squirrel once, right down there in the swamp, with his old shotgun, and he heard that squirrel say, *No, no, don't!*

" 'Twas an easy shot, he said, but he couldn't do it after that. He knew better than to tell anyone but me, though. Times after that, when he'd been prowling, he'd come to me later and say, 'Lou, it happened again,' he'd say. A cottontail rabbit or maybe a raccoon. He figgered out by himself it all came from The Lot, or the woods here, anyway. I tell you, it skeered him! He'd look plumb white afterward. But he'd come back here again and again, just to see if it would keep on happening. Sometimes it did and sometimes it didn't." She paused for breath and locked her hands over her bony knees, rocking back and forth.

"Indian blood could have done it, I guess. They say them things dies hard. A big chief—a sachem, they called them—could maybe talk with animals. They claimed to do all manner of things, and most of it was lies, likely as not. But Jared's long gone, died of the influenza years back, and now there's you. You ain't got no Indian blood?" she asked.

"I don't think so," Alec said.

"So—it must be The Lot. Always was a holy sort of place for the Indians, you know. Kind of like a church is for us. The poor heathen had no other churches."

"I know," Alec said. "Grandpa told me it was a

24

special place and no one could hunt the wild animals here."

"Now then, don't be such a wise-head," Lou said sharply. "Who do you think told him that, for all his book learning and long words? Me, that's who! Not another person in town knows a thing about it. So there!"

Conscious of having reduced her audience of one to silence, she continued, half to herself, half to Alec. "Yes, it's The Lot. I think some people, not just anyone, mind, can get through. Kind of like a one-way telephone. Might be easier for a young 'un, too. Not so much clutter on their minds, so they can hear the critters better, 'specially when they're scairt."

She turned back to Alec and took his nose between two long fingers, tweaking it gently to and fro as she spoke.

"Now look, boy, this here's a secret, all we've spoke about. I want you to tell me if it happens again and I want you not to be frightened. Them little things down there can't hurt nobody, not a soul. I expect all they want is to be let alone. There's nothing to scare you. Think of yourself as lucky and don't tell anyone but me!"

"I won't tell, Lou," he promised. Had it really happened? Surely not. He had imagined it. When Lou went into the house, Alec even allowed himself a small smile. He wouldn't say anything about the skunk's talking. People would think he was crazy!

When Alec finally relaxed on the big sleigh bed in the attic bedroom that night, sleep did not come. He lay and listened to the sounds of the night, the hum of insect life and the whickering of a screech owl, long after the noises downstairs had faded to silence. It was a warm night, and the window was wide open only a few inches from his pillow. The scent of a giant flowering honeysuckle vine, which grew up the side of the old house, poured into the room and the bright stars of early June glittered in the night sky.

He felt more disturbed than ever before in his life. But had the impossible really happened? Alec decided he must believe it had not. People did *not* hear animals talking, regardless of what Lou said. This was the only way to treat the situation.

Eventually, sleep did overcome him. He never saw the great shadow which drifted out of the night an hour later and landed on his window sill, making no more noise than a single feather falling.

He dreamed on as two great yellow eyes stared solemnly at him and blinked and stared and stared and blinked.

2

It seemed to Alec that he had never been asleep, he awoke so quickly. One minute he was dreaming, the next awake, and the transition was so sudden that he almost flew out from under his yellow blanket.

A father robin, who had been teaching his fully-feathered child a few fine points about wing strokes, pushed the startled young bird off the window sill and flew down after it, calling loudly. The sun was on the other side of the house, but light streamed in the windows anyway as the New England day began.

Dressing quickly, Alec raced down the corridor and the back stairs to the kitchen.

"Well," said Lou, turning from the long, iron sink. "I thought the Indians had got out of the TV screen and were charging down the stairs. I see you're awake, anyway."

"Awake enough for three boys, I'd say," said John from the kitchen table, where he had been loafing over a second cup of coffee. It was only seven o'clock, but he had already put in fifteen minutes weeding his

27

garden before breakfast.

"Anything we can do today, John?" said Alec. "Any jobs I can help you with?"

"Not so much of a shout, there, please," said Lou, advancing on him. "You ain't tied your sneakers. And you're going to have breakfast with your grandpa before you go wandering off and getting into trouble with Darden."

When at length Lou had got him looking "decent" and not "like a heathen," she sent him, quieted down a little, back upstairs to brush his teeth and comb his hair.

As he brushed away, he reflected that older people attached far too much importance to neatness and cleanness and made a prompt resolve that he would never brush his teeth when older, but would have them pulled and wear false ones, made of purple glass, so that people would be appalled when he smiled. Finishing his teeth, he ran a comb through his hair and stuck his tongue out at his face in the mirror. Then he ran back downstairs, this time the front way, arriving in the big dining room with a rush and a clatter.

His grandfather, who was wearing an old blue wrapper over his pajamas and carpet slippers, was waiting for him. Once Alec was seated, the Professor reached for the large brass elephant bell in front of his plate and rang it loudly.

Lou entered at once from the pantry, carrying a

tray laden with hot buckwheat pancakes, maple syrup and fresh country sausages, the blend of delightful odors preceding her like a wave.

"Well," said Professor March. "I've been asking for a breakfast like this for months and haven't breached the boiled egg barrier in a cat's age. Do I infer that Alec gets preferential treatment?"

Lou glared at the smiling old gentleman, whom she spoiled in every conceivable way, and answered tartly.

"Alec ain't on no doctor's orders, Professor, and not likely to become an old man with too much weight in front, like some I could name."

"I see that I am once more reduced to silence, a prey to slander in my own house," murmured her opponent. Nevertheless, he seized a healthy portion of the cakes and sausage from the serving plate when it was passed to him. Lou retired to the kitchen, vindicated.

Alec ate voraciously but silently. He knew it was impolite to talk with a full mouth and he wanted to get the food in as soon as possible, because he had thought up a thousand questions that badly needed answering. As a result, he was finished in no time.

"Grandpa," he said suddenly. "Do any wild animals around here bother people? Do they bite people who walk in the woods? Did the old Indians get bitten? Can you get lost in the woods? Are there any big animals? Does anybody *but* animals live there?"

29

"Hold on there! Whoa, take it easy!" said his grandfather. "I haven't even finished eating and I get enough questions to answer in a split-second that would last me all day. Wait 'til I get to my coffee, will you?"

"All right," said Alec, "but I want to go down into the woods and I thought I'd better ask first." He subsided and waited as patiently as he could, staring out of the large rounded windows in the bay at the end of the room at the bright day outside. The light flooded in and the center window was open, although screened, letting in a profusion of sweet odors and a welling chorus of birdsong.

Finally, the Professor's chair scraped back, and he crossed his legs and looked thoughtfully at the boy, stirring his large coffee cup absently as he did so. He spoke now professorially.

"The largest animals you are likely to glimpse will be *Odocoileus virginianus*—the local white-tailed deer, my young zoologist," he said, "and they will take good care to stay out of your way. Still, you may get a look at one, particularly in the evening, near the edge of the pasture.

"A buck in the fall—that's when they mate— can be bad-tempered and ugly; but I never heard of anyone in these parts getting bothered. There hasn't been a painter—that's what they used to call the mountain lion or cougar—in this area since the early 1800's. No bears for nearly that long, either, and no

30

wolves since the eighteenth century, when the locals killed the last ones off. So that takes care of two of your questions.

"Let's see. If my mind functions properly, you wanted to know if anyone but animals lived down in the wood? Presumably you mean people?"

"Yes," said Alec. "Indians maybe, or somebody like that. Somebody who would hide and not want to be found." This was as close as he could come to saying that he had a strange feeling of some presence other than that of the animals out beyond the wall of trees.

"The answer is no," said the old gentleman. "What were you thinking of? We have never had any gypsies in these parts that I know of, and the last Indians left before your great-grandfather was born. Even the old tramps have left the roads and I never heard of a local hermit around here, such as some towns have. As a matter of interest, Alec, the town children don't come out here, although it's not far from the center of Mill Run. I don't discourage them, but they just don't come. Too much to do in town, I imagine.

"The Lot is heavily posted with signs, you know, against hunters and fishermen; and John and I keep a pretty sharp lookout in hunting season. The local people know this. It's been three years since we caught an illegal hunter, and he was a city man.

"Any more questions, or is that it?" he said, as

31

Alec stared past him out the window.

"I asked if any of the animals that were here, the smaller ones, bit people," the boy answered, still thinking over what he had just heard.

"The only danger from any small animal, unless you bother it, of course, is this," said the Professor, "and it's most uncommon. I'm referring to rabies, a very serious and fatal disease that drives animals crazy, and people too, when they get bitten. Dogs catch it, but cats seldom do, for some reason. Move too quickly, I guess.

"Anyway, I never heard of any signs of it in this area. A good rule is to avoid any animal you see acting oddly. If you see a fox, say, stumbling blindly around in daylight or a little bat flying about in the sunlight, bumping into things, or a stray dog with foam around its jaws, then run as quickly as you can and get away from there. But that's all very unlikely. It's something to remember and not worry about, like watching for a green light before you cross the street. Now then, what's left? You know what a porcupine looks like, so don't try to pat one. We get them here once in a great while. The same goes for a skunk. Leave him alone and you'll be fine, because he'll do the same. We have a few copperheads, poisonous snakes. I've never seen one but John has, and even a rattlesnake or two, he tells me. Don't stick your hand into anything you can't see into, like a hole in a stone wall, or under an old log. The rattler is a gentleman, and you'll hear his tail snapping if you're anywhere close. The copperheads are very shy. You practically have to sit down on one before he'll do anything. . . . And that's the whole shebang. Anything more?"

Alec shook his head. He could think of nothing more to ask which would not have come dangerously close to revealing matters better kept to himself.

"Thank you, Grandpa," he said, and got off his chair. "John said he'd take me around. If I think of anything else, I can ask him, can't I?"

"I should think so, and better than me for everything outside," agreed the Professor ungrammatically. "Why, John has more knowledge about this area and what's in it than I do, by a million times. He had the whole place soaked into his bones, and I sometimes think he knows when each blade of grass starts growing." He picked up the morning newspaper as Alec ran from the room and out to the kitchen.

"John is out rambling," Lou informed the boy, "but he's somewhere nearby. Give a good yell," she said firmly, "*outside* the house and that will fetch him."

John appeared at once around the corner of the house in response to Alec's call, carrying a bushel basket and his long, iron spade. Worthless, the cat, orange tail aplume, came padding in his wake.

He grinned at the boy and gestured at him with the basket. "Get your own spade now," he said, "and we'll take a walk down to the brook. Lou makes home-

33

made sarsaparilla, and she can't do it without fresh roots. That means you and me, 'cause somebody's got to dig 'em first."

The spade having been secured, the two strode off through the green-shaded orchard and into the lower pasture, where John led off toward a clearly defined break in the old tumbledown wall. Worthless followed behind.

At the entrance to the wood, however, the big cat ceased to accompany the pair. Planting his fat behind firmly on the earth, he meowed loudly that he was going no further. The cool, green shade which beckoned so invitingly ahead was clearly a barrier to him.

Alec looked down the meandering little path which started at the gap in the wall and then back at the cat before asking:

"John, why doesn't he want to come? Is he scared?"

"Must be," said the man, staring at Worthless. "Come to think of it, he never has liked the woods. Once in a while he'll come in a little ways with me, then he just clears out quick-like and I find him back at the house. Probably met a skunk or something when he was a kitten."

Worthless meowed in apparent agreement and then began washing himself. Without another word, John started off down the path, and Alec followed close behind. Not far inside the shade of the first trees, Alec looked back and saw the cat staring after them. Then a bend in the path hid him from sight, and the boy forgot Worthless as the forest closed around him.

Poplars, tulip trees, great oaks, and maples towered above the heads of the two as they pursued a gentle, winding slope deeper into the heart of the wood. Around them, revealed in flecks of sunlight, the exuberant undergrowth of an uncleared forest had burst from the mat of brown fallen leaves and was struggling for light, the oldest struggle on earth.

Dark green ground pine and lighter mayapple formed patches of blanket-like growth under elder and laurel bushes. Green predominated, but for the white blossoms of the laurel, but there were a thousand shades and permutations of hue, and Alec noticed that no two different plants seemed to have quite the same color. Ferns of every size and tint of green were everywhere.

"Look here, boy," said John, halting and pointing at a lovely, pink flower on a short stem, which grew next to a rotted log.

"That's a moccasin flower. City people call it lady's slipper, and your grandpa told me it's an orchid, related to them they sell in fancy florists. But it looks like an Indian moccasin, don't it now?"

The word "Indian" started a fresh chain of thoughts surging in Alec's mind, and he looked at the beautiful plant in silence, wondering if anything

35

else Indian in nature was still lingering in the forest.

A busy scratching in a pile of leaves to the left of the path drew his attention next, and observing his desire to see the scratcher, John halted and whistled loudly. Out of the leaves appeared a robin-sized bird with a short beak, red breast and a smart black back and tail, fringed with white. It chirped loudly at them. Then it flirted its long tail and plunged back into the leaves, sending them flying and making a loud scrabbling noise.

"Towhee, some call him," said John. "Chewink is what I call him and so do most New Englanders, I guess. Makes enough noise for an elephant for all he's just a little bird looking for bugs. Come on now. If we stop and look at everything, we'll be here til next week, and I've got chores to do besides digging these roots."

There was life all around them, birds flitting from branch to branch, their song exploding in bursts of music, their small shapes showing as they darted from tree to ground or branch to bole. Insects buzzed steadily in a constant background of low-keyed noise.

On the ground itself, small furtive movements seemed never to cease, and its direction was far more purposeful. Alec could never get a clear look at any of it; but walking along behind John, he saw small whiskings and dartings behind trees, going on continually on either side of their line of march. Whenever he tried to pin one of these elusive flurries down, it halted and he would be conscious of another small movement somewhere else.

Once he saw a bright eye staring at him from the depths of a small cluster of wild grape vines; but as soon as the two humans drew close, it vanished. Again, as his head swiveled about, the boy caught the barest flash of motion on the other side of the path, and saw something dark brown and low-slung dart behind a large granite boulder projecting from the leafmold.

John seemed to see none of these things and the boy walked as closely as he could behind him as the old man strode along, slat basket creaking as he swung his arm. But the tiny movements and the sense of being observed never left Alec for a moment. It seemed somehow familiar, recalling something to his mind that he badly wanted to remember. He tried hard to recall what it was, while never failing to notice the shadowy comings and goings with all of his senses.

Winter, that was part of the memory! Now why winter, when it was certainly summer now? A book, that was another part! Winter and a book, he thought, keeping his eye on John's broad, blue shirt back. And —and—faces!

Suddenly, it all came back with a burst of memory. *A narrow little wedge-shaped face.* The Wild Wood in winter! Mole and his desperate flight in *The Wind in the Willows,* which Alec's father had read aloud to him back when he was six. He and John were being followed. If not hunted, they were at least being kept under constant observation by a lot of animals!

This thought was almost too much for him. He had to speak to John, to tell him what he had seen and share the knowledge, as well as gain some comfort.

But he hesitated. Lou's warning had specifically named her husband. Alec had to keep silent. Besides, he thought, perhaps the animals were really doing nothing unusual. Maybe they always followed people. His grandfather had told him that few human beings ever entered the woods. Maybe the little wild things found them merely a new sight, something fun to look at.

Alec swung his spade in a casual way. But deep inside he felt that none of the "maybe's" were true. The animals followed for a purpose; they watched for a purpose; and he, Alec March, was part of that purpose!

But his mind refused to accept this idea and he tramped on, his eye now excluding anything but John Darden's tall form in front of him.

Then a new noise came into his range of hearing, deeper than the birdsong and the muted insect throb. Ahead, John had stopped, and there before them lay Bound Brook.

It ran down through The Lot from the higher land to the west, gurgling in its bed of sand and dark pebble, twisting and turning around mossy boulders and elbows of snow white quartz. Not for nothing is most of Connecticut famous as the rockiest ground in New England, and the stone underlying its surface was clearly visible where the waters of summer and the ice of winter had cut through the soil and deposited leaves of countless years.

"Sit down, boy, and look around," said John, choosing a large, smooth rock for himself. "Nothing prettier than clean water, running through a woods. Take a drink if you want. Like I told you, it's safe, and it tastes better'n any city water you ever had. Got the soil and the trees in it."

"Are there fish?" asked Alec, who was kneeling by the bank, trying to see into the brown depths of a pool which was all of three feet deep.

"Just little minnows, maybe a tadpole or a baby hornpout or madtom—small catfish," said John, peering about for signs of a sarsaparilla plant. "There's some bass and pickerel down in the pond where it's deep, lower on The Lot, but that's got a lot of swamp around it. It's pretty, though, if you can stand a few mosquitoes. I'll take you there later on if you want, but there's a lot of mud."

Alec saw a movement in this particular pool and instantly plunged his bare arm in up to the shoulder. He yelped in surprise a second later and yanked back his arm with a creature like a tiny brown lobster clinging by one claw to his thumb. As his arm left the water, the small animal released its hold, dropped back in with a plop and disappeared, leaving the boy rubbing his pinched finger.

"Ho, hooh," said John, laughing at Alec's indignant face. "Crawdads don't fancy being picked up, now, do they?"

"That hurt!" said Alec, although the soreness was quickly leaving. "Was that a baby lobster, John?"

"Just a crawfish or crawdad, we call them. Good for bait, and not much else. But don't you go a-grabbing everything you see, Alec. A madtom catfish no bigger than that crawdad could give you a poison sting with his fins and your finger would be almighty sore for a week. Best to look before you grab. Now come along and let's find us that sarsaparilla before we forget why we came."

In a short time, he located a clump of short, five-leaved plants with white puffball blossoms and began to dig them up. Alec assisted, and before long the basket was full of the white roots. John cut the leaves and tops off with a large pocket knife.

Alec noticed that wherever they dug, John was careful to fill the holes with leafmold and leave as little trace of their work as possible, always smoothing the ground back as well as he could into its original condition. The leaves of the dug-up plants he buried in one of the holes.

"Alec, if you want a place to look nice and stay the way it ought to be, you try not to make a mess.

Don't leave trash around. Put back what you take out. There's lots of little things can be hurt easy and the more people mess up a pretty place the harder it is to get it back the way it ought to be."

His voice died away in a murmur about "kind of a special place down here, and ought to be kept right."

John hauled a large silver watch from his denim shirt pocket. "I'm going to take these roots back. Some hours still until your lunch time, Alec. Want to come back or stay here? The path is right behind you, so's you can't get lost if you stay by the brook. Or would you rather come back with me?"

Alec wanted to go back, but he also wanted to stay. He was afraid of the forest, but he also felt a sudden tremendous compulsion *not* to leave. A feeling of pressure built up inside his head. Before he knew it, he had said, "I'll poke around right here for awhile," and sat down by the edge of the dancing water.

"Right," said John, shouldering the basket of roots and picking up his spade. "Don't get too wet. Water's still a might cold, but that never hurt a boy in June. Come back up the path when you've a mind to eat, now."

He swung off up the little slope between two laurel bushes and disappeared over a rise almost immediately. And then Alec was alone in the heart of the ancient wood. He looked about nervously. The

41

thought of the animals he had glimpsed on the way down from the meadow returned with full force, but he could see nothing.

Patches of amber sunlight glowed on the leaves and lit clumps of fern and an occasional skunk cabbage. Worn granite boulders, flecked with pale lichens and rock tripe, lay all about, half buried in the dead leaves of the old year. A large red dragonfly darted past to perch on the withered stalk of a wild iris for a second and then hover and flash away down the stream toward its mates on the distant pond.

The pressure, the sense of being expected and even *needed*, which the boy had felt so strongly before John left, had vanished. Instead, he felt relaxed and comfortable. He was conscious only of peace and a desire to rest. Without being at all sleepy, he was yet in no mood to move, but only to sit and stare at the brook. Minutes passed and he still sat, rapt, hugging his spade, his mind idle, transfixed by the melody of the water and the breathing, throbbing background of woodland noises.

The message came as a shock, even though the one bearing it tried to make the transition as easy as possible.

"Turn around and don't be afraid. We have been waiting for you."

The boy stared. Two animals, moving quietly, had emerged from the path behind him and were sitting not six feet away, looking him over as he sat on the bank of the stream.

The one on the left was a large raccoon, grizzled coat and black mask gleaming in a stray sunbeam, black-and-white ringed tail coiled neatly by his side. Alec knew at once that his was the voice he had heard, although how he knew it he could not explain.

The other animal was an enormous old brown woodchuck, who must have weighed at least as much as the raccoon, say thirty pounds, and whose gray muzzle was lifted high in the air as he peered near-sightedly from his small eyes. Great square front teeth, yellow with age, showed as he wrinkled his nose at intervals.

"Now don't go jumping around like a silly grass-hopper," came the voice again. "We have to talk to you at once, and we aren't going to hurt you. Or you us," he added.

The blood throbbed in Alec's temples and he remained unmoving on the ground as if rooted there. Everything in his body seemed numb and he could hardly breathe.

"And put that spade down!" The animal stirred irritably, shifting his weight on his plump haunches.

Alec relaxed and obeyed, although he kept the spade at his side.

"That's better," said the raccoon. "You have a lot to learn in a short time and nobody can learn any-thing if they're scared half to death. Now just be sensible. This isn't easy for us, either, you know. I can talk to you but it's hard. You can't talk to me yet, because you don't know how. That takes learning. So simply relax and it will all go more smoothly."

Despite his astonishment, Alec could not help being fascinated. Just as in his previous encounter with the skunk, the conversation was clear, although it seemed to come to him almost instantaneously.

"Call me Scratch," said the raccoon. "This is Stuffer," he added, indicating the big woodchuck. "Say something to the human, stupid."

"Hello," said Stuffer slowly. To Alec the wood-chuck's "voice" was totally different from the quick conversation of the raccoon, being heavy and labored, quite like the clumsy-looking animal himself.

"We don't have names, like you humans," said the raccoon, "but you have to call us something. Stuffer never stops eating unless he's asleep, and I'm always scratching something up. I thought of Washer," he added, "but I don't really wash all of my food, so Scratch is better."

"I'm not eating now," said the thick woodchuck voice suddenly, "and I'm not asleep, either. What's *his* name, anyway, or does he know it?"

"Aha," said the raccoon. "Glad you woke up. Of course he has a name, but he can't say it to us. That's why we're here, remember?"

He directed his attention back to Alec and moved a few feet closer. The boy felt his fear ebbing away as he watched. The animals were obviously not about to harm him.

The raccoon sat down again and looked up at him.

"You have to talk to us, too," he said. "Try and tell us your name."

"I'm Alec!" the boy said loudly.

Both the animals visibly flinched. The raccoon, Scratch, raised one paw in protest. "Not so loud, for goodness' sake," he said. "All we get is a tremendous noise that doesn't mean a thing. You don't have to talk by using *noise,* you know. We don't."

It was true, Alec noted in amazement. Although the animal's conversation sounded clearly in his mind, they were not speaking to him with words at all.

"Try again, but not so hard."

The boy shut his eyes to concentrate better, and tried to think his name.

"No good," came a grunt from the woodchuck. "He's trying, I will say, but it doesn't tell me anything."

"Nobody thought this would be easy," retorted the raccoon. "Give him a chance. A beaver dam wasn't built in a day, as the saying goes." He sent another thought to Alec.

"What do you like to do best, human? Try thinking of yourself doing that, whatever it is."

Alec thought hard and finally decided he liked playing with, or watching, animals. He was nervous about thinking of himself at the zoo or museum (for fear of hurting feelings), but he tried to think of the zoo as having no bars and the animals in the museum as being alive.

"Hm, huh, hmm," came the rough voice of Stuffer. "I think I'm getting something now. He likes to look at animals, I think. No metal sticks or killing things, just looking. A nice enough young human, I guess."

"We already knew that," said Scratch brusquely. "Why do you think he was picked? But it gives me an idea. We can call him Watcher. Now, Watcher," he went on, "think of yourself, a picture of you, watching an animal. Can you do that?"

Alec tried to fix his mind on seeing himself standing watching a raccoon. In his thought he removed all background so that only he and the animal appeared in his thoughts. *Watcher. I am Watcher.*

"Not bad," said Scratch. "Did you get that, you rooteater?" he threw in for the woodchuck's benefit. "He's trying hard and it's coming through. Almost as good as one of my own young ones!"

"All right, all right," said Stuffer. "But all he's said is his own name. We need a lot more than that." Alec heard all of this, of course, and flushed with shame. The human irony of being jibed at by a woodchuck never occurred to him. He just felt badly about not being able to do better at something the animals seemed able to do so easily.

"Try again," said Scratch patiently. "Give us your

name picture. Good. That came over clearly. Now try something harder. What did you eat this morning?"

The boy tried.

"Round meat things and flat cakes, I got that faintly."

Now it was Stuffer's turn to defend Alec. "He's just learning," said his slower tones. "All young animals talk blurry when they're starting, Scratch."

"I know," said the raccoon, "but he's making my head itch!"

The practice went on. After about an hour of learning to send out simple pictures, such as those of his family, his belongings, and the house up on the hill, Alec began to feel more confident.

By this time the woodchuck and the raccoon were sitting right next to him, and at times were actually pawing his legs when they wanted to emphasize something or became impatient. Around them the rest of the wood went on about its regular business, the birds and insects behaving as usual, the sun shining down through the green canopy of leaves overhead and light breezes ruffling the tops of the trees.

But below on the ground, the three figures remained intent and preoccupied, paying no attention to anything else except what they were doing. The white shirt stayed bent over the two small pointed heads and they in turn kept their eyes fixed on the human face staring down into theirs.

Alec had now attained a limited ability to send two

or three pictures at once. While not yet ready to "talk" on the same level as Scratch and Stuffer, he could at last ask questions. He had discovered that the easiest way to do this was to make a picture and then make his mind a total blank immediately afterwards. While not as fast as human speech, at least as yet, he learned that he could still find out a good deal.

"What do you eat?" Alec asked Stuffer. He thought about a picture of a bare patch of earth and the woodchuck sitting in front of it.

Back came a series of pictures of grass, roots, leaves and fallen fruit.

"What about you?" The boy turned to Scratch. This time the list was far longer. It included items ranging from green corn to frogs and mice, which gave rise to still more questions.

"Do raccoons and woodchucks always go around together?" Alec did this by showing Scratch and Stuffer with a wall between them.

This last question made the two creatures terribly excited, and they both began to "talk" so fast that Alec could hardly understand them. Conflicting pictures poured into his mind. But he had picked up a lot in the time he had already spent learning, and he was able to grasp, after a good deal of hard effort, most of what they were saying.

Apparently the local animals were acting very strangely, and were not fighting and hunting as they usually did. In the ordinary way of things, a raccoon and a woodchuck had nothing at all to do with one another, nor did a skunk and a fox. Deer and mice had even fewer interests in common, any more than did birds and animals that lived on the ground or in holes.

But now this normal state of things was all upset. All, or at least most, of the resident forest people had buried their past animosities. The hunting animals, such as the foxes, all hunted outside The Lot, as far away as possible, and did not disturb any of their small neighbors. Squirrels had stopped robbing the local birds' nests; and the big birds of prey, such as owls and hawks, hunted miles away from their home territories.

A complete and very effective truce was in fact being carried on both night and day throughout the whole length and breadth of The Lot. The two animals were quivering with nervous energy and delight when Alec made it plain that he finally understood all this.

Of course, the next question was obvious. Why? And the boy asked it, without realizing how hard such a question is to ask with pictures. But he did it without even thinking and actually, as he later learned, very rudely by showing Scratch and Stuffer fighting. Then he showed them sitting side by side in a "question" picture.

But the two simply would not, or could not, tell him the answer. They did tell him something else.

"Can you get out at night?" said Scratch, resting a long-clawed front paw on Alec's knee. "Can you come out to the wood and see us here—tonight? It's very important. We have to see you, but we can't tell you why right now."

The big raccoon's black eyes seemed to implore the boy to say yes.

Alec stiffened in dismay at the question. The thought of where he should be that night, secure in the big sleigh bed, brought back the human world he had left. Go out at night? Leave the house, come down here to the dark wood alone, in the pitch black?

"Don't be scared," said the woodchuck. "We'll meet you. There is nothing to be frightened of in the dark. All of us will watch you and guide you."

"Yes," Scratch said. "There is nothing to fear. We need you badly. To help us. But we must see you at night. You can rest in the afternoon, and then you won't need to sleep tonight. But you simply must come. We two will wait near the house, and the minute you get close, we'll be beside you. There's nothing wrong with being out at night."

Alec relaxed a bit as he stared at the two earnest and pleading faces. He was both frightened and attracted at the same time. It was nice to know that he was needed, for whatever it was. His sneaker scuffed a clump of small pink mushrooms idly, and Stuffer promptly leaned over and gathered them up with his small front paws. He began to eat them in gulps and

50

the sight of the bulging cheek pouches and busy face made Alec laugh.

Scratch was quick to note the change in his manner. "You'll come, won't you?" he said, anxious to take advantage of the boy's happier mood. "It's terribly important!" His whole body quivered and the ringtail fluffed up like a round brush. "You will, won't you?"

"I think so," said Alec slowly. "I'm not supposed to go out at night, and I'm sure I'm not supposed to come down here. Suppose someone hears me?" He was so wrapped up in what he was saying that he never realized that he had passed the last "language" test. He was now "talking" to the two animals almost as freely, if not quite as quickly, as they were to him.

"You must be quiet, that's all," grumbled the woodchuck. "Can't you go quietly down from where you sleep, like one of us?"

"Everything will be ruined if the big humans find out," added Scratch. "We can't talk to them. You're the first human any of us has talked to in—in—well in so long a time we've almost forgotten how. Once there were people here, not like you, with different colored skin, and they talked to us. But only a few of us remembered this and it was many, many lives ago." He did not say "years ago," but Alec understood him. Alec also understood what was said about the long-vanished Indians, better even than the two animals did, for of course he knew more.

A sudden interruption brought all three to rigid

51

attention. Down the wind, and over the forest noises came a wailing call, the sound of a human voice. "Alec, A-a-a-lec! Lunch ti-i-i-ime!" Even at that distance, it was readily identifiable to the boy as a summons from Lou.

"I have to go," he said quickly. "But I'll try to come tonight. But I don't know how, or when I can sneak out."

"We'll wait in the apple orchard," messaged Scratch, and Stuffer mumbled agreement. "We'll wait all night if we have to. But if you can, come as soon as it's dark."

Alec was already running up the path as the last words came through. He stopped at the turn and looked back. The two animals sat up on their hind legs, staring after him. Something imploring in their manner touched his heart. Mentally, he vowed that he would get out that night, somehow.

He ran on, panting a little, and soon burst out of the edge of the woods and into the open pasture.

Up at the edge of the last fruit trees he saw Lou, who waved at the sight of him, and he was suddenly conscious of being both tired and very hungry.

Behind him, the forest lay silent, even the bird voices hushed in the heat of noon.

3

From his open window, Alec could just see the brow of the hill behind the house and the upper pasture outlined in the sunset's afterglow. A few scattered dwarf cedars, one of the few that will grow on worn-out New England soil, stood in black clumps in the field, their feet already hidden in the shadows of oncoming night.

From deep in the distant wood there came faintly the liquid notes of a veery, the loveliest singer and shyest of all the forest-haunting thrushes. Aside from scattered bird voices and the buzz of insects, the stillness of late evening lay on the softened landscape.

Earlier, Lou Darden had not scolded him for dawdling in the woods and being late for lunch. She had seemed rather to be pleased that he had enjoyed himself, and had asked many questions about what he had seen. She had made it quite plain that she wanted to know if he had been frightened again, or had had any strange encounter such as that of the previous day.

Alec did not like to lie and was strongly tempted to tell her all that had happened, but he remembered, just in time, that he would have to tell her also what his plans for the evening were, and he knew very well what her answer to that would be! And so he had given a totally fictitious account of how he had spent the morning unsuccessfully trying to catch small fish in Bound Brook. This seemed to satisfy her, and she asked no more questions.

Alec had eaten two huge cheese sandwiches, a bowl of soup, a glass of milk and a piece of apple pie; and then he had gone quietly upstairs and lain down, for he was quite tired. Lou was not in the least suspicious and later told Darden that she thought the fresh air was doing wonders for the boy, but that he needed more rest.

Alec spent the afternoon out of sight of the house, simply continuing his rest in the shade of a dogwood tree on the edge of the orchard, not seeing either Darden or his wife. He had loafed the long afternoon away, occasionally rousing enough to hear the sound of John's hoe in the garden lower down on the hill. Once he had wakened sharply to find a soft, warm body pressed against him, but realized immediately that it was only Worthless, who had sought him out to use as a pillow.

Struck by an idea, he had tried for some minutes to communicate mentally with the big cat, but had got absolutely nowhere. The fat, whiskered face and great yellow eyes stared blankly back at him, and gave no sign of either interest or response. In fact, after a moment or two, Worthless fell asleep and even his deep, rumbling purr ceased entirely.

This actually did not surprise the boy. It seemed plain to him that only wild animals, and perhaps not all of them, possessed the ability to talk. He simply accepted this fact without question. Worthless couldn't talk and there it was: a simple matter, nothing to get upset about.

The warm afternoon had lazed on and so had Alec, in a pleasant dreamy state halfway between sleeping and waking. His plans were all made and it was only a matter of passing the time. He knew that he needed rest. He tried, not unsuccessfully, to keep his thoughts away from the night ahead, and although it was hard, he got through the afternoon somehow.

He ate with his grandfather by request, since the old gentleman was hungry earlier than usual. They had a very good time. The Professor possessed reams of information on a thousand subjects and sometimes forgot, during a long speech about something or other, that he was not addressing a learned audience or arguing with a former university colleague. This suited Alec perfectly, since he could merely listen and extract fascinating words and not really have to answer at all. That evening, he had learned that something called "caltrops," devices apparently made for hurting horses, were a much underrated weapon in the Middle Ages. Also, that a good deal of field work was needed to solve the very real problem of the "Irish dispersal to Iceland." And finally, that Richard the Lionheart (one person Alec had actually heard of before) was a bad man and a bad king, worse perhaps even than his brother, King John, whom everyone thought so evil. . . .

But now here Alec was, waiting for the last light to die and dark night to come. The stars were out and the full moon had appeared. The frogs in the distant swamp had begun to call, and a few more insect buzzings hummed in the air as night drew on. Alec sniffed a clump of honeysuckle blossoms which peeped over the sill and tried to see if he could spot any trace of light still left in the sky. It was ten o'clock by the chimes of the hall clock.

"Are you ready?" said a voice in his mind. He almost fell off the window ledge as he bounced erect and jumped back. He could see nobody.

"I'm on the vine," said the voice. "Don't be afraid, Watcher, I've come to take you outside to the others." It was a new voice, one he had never heard, he realized at once. It conveyed a touch of lightness and delicacy, of someone quick and dancing. And something else, too. As he fought to make his heart stop pounding and get his breath back, he realized that it was this difference which startled him the most. The raccoon and the woodchuck had been so clearly male that the first *female* animal voice in his mind was a real shock. Why, this was a lady!

As he stared at the window, something very small moved there, and he realized that he had been looking right at it for several seconds, but missing it because of its size.

"Call me Whisperfoot," said the voice, and as the boy moved slowly forward, the tiny creature came out further from the vine and sat looking at him. It was a mouse.

For some seconds, the two stared at each other without speaking. Whisperfoot was a white-footed, or woodland, deermouse. She had a snow-white belly, legs and feet, while the rest of her was a warm red-dish-brown color, save for the large, pink shell-like ears and the long tail. She looked incredibly neat and tidy, and gave Alec an instant feeling that his hair wasn't combed, or his face washed.

"Well," said her tinkling mind-voice at length, "are you scared of me?" There was just a hint of laughter in the voice and Alec blushed as he caught it.

"Hello," he said slowly. "Did you say I was coming with you? I don't think I can, climbing down that vine. I'd fall."

Again there was a hint of elfin laughter in her voice. "No, we didn't think you could climb that well. I'm going with *you*. That is," she added demurely, "if you don't mind carrying me. I can ride on your shoulder and tell you where to go."

Alec considered. He could creep downstairs, carrying his wee guest, and go out the side door in the library, which he had carefully left unlatched that afternoon. And now that he would have a companion, the whole trip no longer seemed so frightening.

"Okay," he said. "I guess I'm ready if you are." He came closer and gently laid his hand on the window sill. Quick as a flash, Whisperfoot was up his arm and onto his shoulder. She was so light that he could hardly feel her tiny feet through the cloth of the T-shirt.

Scratch had decided to leave nothing to chance in his scheme to get Alec out to the wood. The wise raccoon had sensed the boy's fear. Knowing that an animal the size of a mouse could hardly be a fright to anyone, he had issued a call for volunteers to some of his small allies, and the young deermouse, only a half-year old and with no family, had bravely said that she would go.

The whole idea had worked exactly as Scratch had hoped. Alec felt heartened and he also felt protective. He realized that it was a tremendously heroic thing for such a little creature to place herself at the mercy of a strange human giant a hundred times her size, who could crush her by a mere wave of one hand. He resolved that she would not regret coming to him.

"I'll take my spade," he said to her. "Then if anything bothers us, I'll whack him over the head!"

"Don't do that," she answered. "The other animals

might be afraid of it. And no one will bother us, unless it's that yellow cat you humans keep here. And he's so stupid and slow a blind beetle could get away from him. You can hear him breathing a mile away, he's so fat," she added contemptuously.

Alec was amused at the description of poor Worthless, for he saw that to a wild, free creature, the bulky tomcat would probably look pretty funny.

"All right," he answered. "Shall we go?"

"Yes, let's hurry. There's a lot to do tonight and we have to go down deep into the wood where all the others are waiting at the Council Glade."

Alec felt a return of uneasiness when she said "deep into the wood" and "all the others," but he fought it down gamely. After all, he had done a lot of thinking since the morning, and it was plain that Scratch and Stuffer had not just been speaking for themselves, but for a lot of other animals as well. Whisperfoot's presence on his shoulder was a clear proof of that.

He tiptoed over and opened his bedroom door. Whisperfoot thought he was terribly noisy, but then no wild creature thinks a human is properly quiet. Actually, Alec made very little sound (he had tied two knots in each of his sneakers earlier, to prevent loose shoelaces) and he passed into the long upper hall like a shadow.

Down the hall from the Dardens' sitting room came the faint sound of a television set in action, an occasional popping noise indicating that Western bad-men and heroic marshals were conducting their nightly gun duels for Lou and John's benefit.

The hall was dark except for a thin line of light under the Dardens' door. The hall windows, opening on the outside of the house, were merely patches a lighter shade of gray than the rest of the wall. The entrance to the front stairwell loomed like a black pit just in front of them. No noise or light were apparent from the ground floor.

Silently, Alec padded to the head of the stairs and started down. A pinch of claws on his shoulder told him that the mouse was not quite as brave as she had made out to be.

Halfway down the stairs, on the landing where they turned, he stopped and listened, all of his senses alert. He could see the library door, slightly ajar, with no light behind it, and at the sight he realized that he had completely forgotten his grandfather in his calculations. Where was the old gentleman? Asleep in his chair in the library? Wandering around the house? Outside, having a walk in the cool night air? Alec's heart almost stopped as he wondered what to do.

"What's the matter?" came the crystal mind voice of his companion. "Why are you scared again?"

"It's my grandfather," said Alec, feeling miserable. "I forgot to figure out where he'd be. If he catches me, I'll never get out."

"Hmm," said the mouse thoughtfully. "Is that the old human with the white fur on his head? If it is, you need better ears, Watcher. He won't bother us. Listen!"

A long muffled snore, which Alec had been hearing without even realizing it ever since he had left his bedroom, echoed clearly down the upper hall from the master suite occupied by the Professor. Having eaten early, he had probably decided to retire early as well.

Alec stole down the rest of the stairs and into the library, shutting the door gently behind him. He wondered for a second when he would get back, then headed for the French doors opening onto the side lawn.

As he eased one of the doors open, the fresh, scented air of the summer night cooled his face. He took a deep breath and then walked out of the house and stood for a moment under the stars.

"Whew!" said Whisperfoot in relief. "Now we're safe, with nothing to worry about." Alec realized for the second time that she had been really terrified inside the house, and again he appreciated how brave she had been.

"I'll look after you," he said. "Don't worry. I can punch anyone on the jaw who bothers us."

"No one needs to look after me," she said somewhat crossly. "I'm just glad to be away from all those nasty smells. I don't see how you humans live with them. I thought I'd choke before I got out."

"But we have mice in the house already," said Alec without thinking.

"Mice, indeed!" came back the angry answer. "Those dirty little things? They don't even come from around here. They followed you humans from some horrid place over the big salt water, and all they can do is live in your houses and steal your leftover food. And the dirt they live in!" Her thoughts expressed the dislike that a wild leopard might feel for a poor alley cat, covered with mange. It was a contempt mixed with pity and a little sorrow, that an animal could so lower itself as to both be dirty and deliberately live with humans. To an untamed woods animal, always spotlessly clean and living on freshly-gathered food, the humble likes of a house mouse seemed beneath contempt.

"Come on, Watcher," she said, as Alec still stood by the wall of the house. "We have a long way to go. The others are waiting out under the last apple tree."

Reluctantly, the boy moved away from the building and out across the lawn. He crouched a little and quickened his pace as he left the house, finally breaking into a run as he headed for the nearest trees in the orchard. He felt that numerous eyes were peering out of the night, all directed at the center of his back.

Once under the shadow of the first big Seckel pear tree, he stopped, his heart pounding with the sudden excitement.

"Why are you stopping?" came the mouse's voice.

"Come on, now, hurry up, or we'll be late. Straight ahead, out to the edge of the orchard and that last big tree."

His white shirt showing momentarily as he dashed from tree to tree, Alec worked his way out in the direction Whisperfoot had indicated. Finally, one lone tree, a giant aged apple tree, its outer branches sweeping the ground, lay before them. His sight by now perfectly attuned to the dappled moonlight, the boy stared around him from the shade of another tree. The starlight made fine details hard to pick out, but he could see clearly the slope of the meadow and the way it fell toward the old wall. Black and grim a quarter of a mile away, the forest reared like some impenetrable wall a shade darker than the night sky, the tops of the trees barely outlined against the stars.

The scent of clover and other meadow flowers mingled with the pungent odor of wild onion in Alec's nose. Wet grass, soaked with early dew, brushed his knees. He unconsciously quieted his breathing and tried also to stop his heart from pounding. He knew that once he had crossed the patch of pale meadow to the last tree, that there would be no going back.

"Just relax," Whisperfoot said, her delicate voice seeming to chime like a tiny bell in Alec's head. "We are all your friends, remember? Nothing can hurt you while we are all here."

He rushed out of the shadows and scuttled under the branches of the big apple tree, where he came to a halt by the trunk. Two dim shapes rose from the ground at the base of the tree to greet him.

"Good," said the remembered mind-voice of Scratch. "I see she got you here, and earlier than we expected." A clearly audible sound of chewing and a mental grunt indicated that Stuffer had, as usual, been storing up food against any contingency.

"Nobody brought him!" retorted Whisperfoot sharply. "He brought himself, and me, too, for that matter. He's a very brave person and you don't have to sound so pleased with yourself. I'd like to have seen you when you were young. Probably spent all night hiding in a hole in some hollow tree with your stripey tail over your face!"

The raccoon chuckled. "I see he's made a new friend, anyway, which is all to the good. Not that we're not *all* his friends," he added hastily. "Still, you can't have too many. Let's get moving. I'll go in front and warn you of any branches or stones. Stuffer, stop eating those weeds and bring up the rear. Look sharp, now!"

"Wait," said Alec suddenly. "I'm not scared, but I have to know something. How late will it be when I get back? I can't come back when it's daylight. You have to bring me back while it's still night. And where are we going?"

"If we stand here all night," said Scratch impatiently, "we'll never get back. We thought of all this before. Humans aren't the only creatures with brains, you know. You'll be back in plenty of time, but we have to get moving."

"All right," said Alec. "I'm ready. Go ahead."

In single file, which is how almost all animals travel, the little party went out into the open and headed for the woods. The raccoon and the woodchuck, both being short-legged creatures, humped up in the middle as they flowed over the ground, but they still moved briskly along.

Alec found that he had, without realizing it, put his right hand up on his shoulder and curled it around his passenger in a protective way. "Don't worry about me," she said. "I can move pretty fast when I have to. But thanks anyway." He noticed that the raccoon was not aiming for the break in the wall which he and John had used that morning, but instead was angling further downhill, to a place where the wall bent to the right and headed for the driveway to the house. It was toward this corner that they were going.

They came to the angle and Scratch promptly scrambled over the loosely piled stones and vanished into the blackness of the trees overhanging the wall. From ahead, his voice came back to them. "There's a path here and nothing to climb but the wall. Come ahead."

Alec carefully examined the wall, and saw what he felt sure was poison ivy, growing over one large rock. This he avoided and climbed over carefully, using both hands to balance. Behind them, he heard the scratch of claws and a low grunt, to indicate that Stuffer was still following in the rear. Ahead the thick darkness seemed impossible to see through, and he almost jumped when a paw touched his foot.

"I'm right here, and I'll still go in front," said Scratch. "Walk slowly and keep one hand in front of your eyes, in case a branch swings down that I don't see. There's a narrow path here, but it goes quite straight for a long way. If we come to any obstacles, I'll warn you."

They were standing at the entrance to a deer trail, used by these larger animals when they came out to the upper meadow at night to feed on the grass and fallen fruit. Like all such trails, it was quite clear but very narrow, permitting only one deer at a time to pass along it. Alec stepped out hesitantly, one arm up, and cautiously began to walk forward. As he gained confidence, he was able to see better and he realized that even here, under the overhead canopy of leaves, there was some dim light, however filtered and dwindled. The eyes of his companions had no such difficulty, for of course they were all three animals who went abroad at night and slept through much of the day.

They went down a long, gentle slope in silence, save for the murmur of the breeze in the trees high above them and the rustle of leaves under Alec's feet. He noticed that even the awkward-looking woodchuck made very little noise, while Scratch might have been

66

walking on air for all the sound his feet caused. Occasionally his voice would send a message to the boy's mind, of a stump near the path, or a low branch; but Alec could now see so well that most of these warnings were unnecessary. Once the raccoon warned of a cat-claw vine across the path and Alec lifted his feet over the thin, spiny bramble, which he could not see in the dark. Other than that, their steady march was uninterrupted.

The faint frog voices, which had sounded quite noisy, though distant, from the second floor of the house, had died away and become almost inaudible when they first entered the forest. Now they gradually began to grow louder again. The earth underfoot was softer, and Alec had the feeling that they were coming to water. The air felt moister and the ground had leveled off, as if the group had left the slope of the hill and was now advancing on the flat.

As the frog chorus grew, Alec became conscious of yet other sounds. Small, muted cracklings and soft rustlings sounded from either side of the path, and he was quick to remember his trip to the woods in the morning. It was the sound of many other creatures accompanying the little group, and despite their care, their numbers were betrayed by the noise of their passage. Once again, the boy's fears returned. What was he getting into?

"They are all going to the same place we are," came the voice of Whisperfoot. "Don't be nervous now. Nobody wants to hurt you. We all want you to help us, and you can't do that if you let yourself be frightened." She had sensed his rising panic and her soothing message helped to calm him down.

Ahead of him now, his night eyes began to see more light. The full moon had risen yet higher, adding its pale strength to the dim starshine.

An open glade became gradually visible, ringed by tall trees, mostly oak and pine, and the little path was leading directly into it. The frog chorus was quite loud now, and Alec decided that the clearing must be located quite close to the pond. Tall, damp grass brushed his thighs as he followed the dimly-seen form of the raccoon out into the open. Once inside the clearing, he stopped and looked around. He found that he was able to see quite well and the sight held him enthralled.

The entire area was filled with secret movement. Small bodies were packed in wherever they could fit, larger creatures looming over them, and all were shifting restlessly about, as if they could not stay still but had to keep in continual motion. In the pale moonlight, Alec saw two red foxes quite near him, side by side and staring calmly at him as they stood, shifting their dainty feet occasionally in little dancing steps. A whole swarm of cottontail rabbits, adults and young, the latter only the size of large mice, were crouched around the foxes, paying no attention to them at all. Almost at the boy's feet, a gray opossum, its long naked tail catching the faint light, ambled slowly through a horde of meadow mice like a battle tank moving through a restless sea of infantry soldiers. Further off, Alec saw the black-and-white gleam of two skunks, and wondered if one of them was the animal he had seen, whose mind voice he had heard the day before.

Turning his head, he now saw to his left some large pale patches of movement, so large, indeed, that he almost started in amazement. His eyes were used to taking in smaller creatures and the realization that he was seeing a whole herd of deer not thirty feet away left him shaken. The big animals, at least a dozen at a guess, were keeping to the edge of the wood in an effort to avoid crushing the smaller beasts which filled the glade almost to overflowing. But they, too, were drifting back and forth, a prey to nervous energy and excitement.

And aside from the rustle of countless feet there was not a sound! Not the youngest mouse or smallest chipmunk baby made a squeak. Only the scuffing of the grass and the soft susurration of animal bodies in movement broke the quiet of the night. Even the frogs had suddenly stopped their croaking from the nearby pond. The hum of tiny insect voices and the drone of a mosquito or two were the only exceptions. The whole night seemed to wait.

But Alec felt something else now, and didn't like it at all. There was a new sense of pressure and heaviness in his head, a feeling that a swarm of bees had got inside his mind and were flying around banging into things, trying to get out and not succeeding. With every second this feeling became stronger and stronger, until he could actually feel a sharp pain in his temples. Forgetting the marvels all around him, he gasped, his hands going up to his throbbing head. It felt now as if his head were in a great press, which was steadily and remorselessly crushing it. Then, just when he was about to scream and throw himself on the ground, so terrible had the hurt become—it suddenly ceased.

He stood, swaying slightly, his head ringing like a bell from the cessation of pressure, but the pain was gone. And all about him he was conscious of utter and total silence. A thousand eyes were fixed upon him, but nothing moved. From the largest whitetail buck to the newest mouse child in the grass, not a creature stirred. "Not even a mouse," he thought absurdly.

The voice of Scratch came into his mind. "Sorry, Watcher. They have all been waiting for you and they got so excited that they all began to think at you and try and catch your thoughts in return. Pretty bad, wasn't it? They didn't mean to hurt you and when I saw what was happening, I made them stop. They all want to say they're sorry and it won't happen again. How do you feel now?"

"I'm all right, I guess," said Alec, shaking his

head to make it stop ringing. "Can they hear me when I talk to you? Boy, that really hurt, what they did."

"Yes," said the raccoon. "They can hear, but they won't try to talk again, unless it's one at a time. Don't worry. This is just as new to them as it is to you. No one had talked to a live human, except by accident, for so long that the whole forest didn't believe it could be done, or even ever *had* been done, for that matter. Now they know better. Can't you feel the difference?"

He could. There was no longer any hurt or pressure, but he caught a strange feeling in his mind, as if a great soft blanket had arisen from the earth and flowed gently over him, warming and soothing at the same time. It was a very comforting feeling and he knew that he was not in any danger from the multitude of creatures gathered around him. But he was not to be given long to think about it.

"Come with me," said Scratch. The raccoon began to move forward toward the center of the circle and the animals that stood between him and his goal parted, making a narrow path. Hesitantly, the boy followed him, watched by countless eyes as he came further out into the open.

"Put me down now," came a thought message from Whisperfoot. "You have to go out in the middle by yourself. I'll see you again afterward." Alec stooped and laid one arm gently on the warm earth.

The shadowy shape of the deermouse darted down his arm and vanished into a sea of small creatures to the right of the open path. Then the boy stood up again and followed Scratch, his feet steady but his heart hammering.

The big raccoon stopped finally near the middle of the clearing and waited for Alec to catch up. As he drew close, Alec saw that a circular space in the exact center of the Council Glade had been left clear. A ring of animal faces surrounded it on all sides, but none encroached upon it.

There, the grass was clipped like a lawn, the blades only an inch high. In the middle of the smooth grass was a circle of large, smooth, flat stones, hardly protruding from the ground. They in turn guarded a space about five feet square, where the lawn was so closely trimmed that no individual grasses could be seen at all. As Alec approached, Scratch moved to one side and his voice came into the boy's brain.

"Go out to the middle, between those flat rocks, lie down, and shut your eyes. Nothing will hurt you, but it has to be done this way. Don't be afraid."

"I'm not afraid," said Alec. And he wasn't. He felt a compulsion to go forward which had nothing to to do with the animals any longer.

He had been called, his presence had been demanded, by something as far removed from the creatures around him as an ant is removed from a star. Something ancient and wise, a force as undefined and mighty as a hurricane and yet as placid and inflexible as a giant tree, was beckoning.

The soul of the ancient wood had waked after long years of dreaming, and had summoned a human for purposes of its own. Without the slightest bit of fear, Alec walked through the ring of flat rocks, lay down and folded his arms across his chest. He closed his eyes.

A gray mist seemed to cover his thoughts. He seemed to walk in a cloud of haze and smoke which shifted and drifted constantly. All feelings of heat and cold were gone, as were the senses of smell and hearing.

Then the mind-mist began to thin and there appeared a Face.

He could never quite be sure, in later times, whether it was human or animal. It seemed to change somehow between the two. Now it was the bronzed head of a huge Indian warrior, long braided plaits of black hair hanging over the ears, painted bars of color on the broad cheek bones, black jetty eyes staring into his. Then suddenly, the human aspect would leave it completely and the appearance of a giant tawny cat would be poised in the fog, the yellow eyes with their dark slitted pupils drilling into his mind as if in search of his most secret thoughts.

Then back would come the head of the great Indian, only to be replaced by the mask of a huge wolf, with long gray muzzle, pointed ears cocked, and white grinning fangs. And always the eyes never left his and the Face itself hung motionless, poised in nothingness. It might have been gigantic and a hundred miles away in space or normal in size and only a few yards distant.

Alec felt himself caught up in the tide of great forces, forces long sleeping and quiet. A test was being given him, far more thorough than any he had experienced. His memories, his most hidden thoughts, were being probed and turned over, held up to an outside scrutiny and then gently replaced. A vast intelligence, beyond human comprehension, was studying the mental pictures it had extracted from his brain. And all the while, as Alec felt the power of the mind, he also felt its age.

For it was old beyond the meaning of the word, born in an age so remote as to make all human history seem only a second in time.

At last, after what seemed hours to Alec, a loosening came of the invisible bond which held him fixed in the place of swirling clouds. A voice, tremendous and vibrant, seemed to fill the whole universe like the strokes of some great bell.

"I have called you, young human, to come before my Gate. Are you afraid?"

Alec answered, but not as he had talked to the animals. Rather he spoke in his human voice, or it seemed to him that he did.

"I'm not afraid. Why am I here? Who are you?"

"I have many names," said the voice, which rolled and echoed in his mind like thunder over distant mountain peaks. "Once I was called Manibozo by a red people who have since dwindled and passed away. I have many Gates, of which this is the least, and moreover one long unused. I live both in your world and outside, coming and going as I choose.

"Many Gates and many names have I, and all the life of your human world is little to me, who was here first, as I shall be last. For I have no longer anything to do with your race or kind. From out of the past, beyond the memory of the first of your people who ever lived, I came, who had been here long ages before the red race came from over the western seas to hunt the hairy elephant and the giant sloth.

"And when all are gone I shall still be here, who belong to the land and the beasts, the rocks and the trees, the waters and the wind. For a time the life of the world may forget me; but always I return and always the land is here and always are the seasons renewed.

"I have been worshipped as a god. But I am no god, but only one of the first things to come alive and breathe and move in all this wide earth. The animals have named you 'Watcher.' Well, I am one of the Watchers of Eternity, and all the forests and lakes and plains and mountains, and all that live therein are my concern. In other lands beyond the great oceans are others of my kind, and in the seas are more. But here I am the First, who have guarded the life of this land since before the mountains were young and newborn, and a helpless, gasping thing struggled across the mud to gain a distant pool, knowing not that its clumsy fins were the first legs.

"At this late day my people, the little forest creatures around you, have remembered my forgotten Gate in this glade where once the red-skinned folk used to pray for my aid. And I have listened and harkened and I have come. I have told them that you are one who may help them. For against men and their works I can do nothing." The voice paused for a moment, and a strange note of sadness crept into it.

"Men have their own Judge and their own perils and it is given to other hands than mine to balance their evil and their good. Men answer to Another and on their day of reckoning I will not be there, unless as a witness.

"A peril threatens my forest people here and also my long-forgotten Gate. And the menace is one which comes from the same source as do I, and to meet it falls within the authority I was given in ages past."

A note of humor, vast and ironic, came into the voice. "But I must call upon a human to aid the small folk of tree and earth. I offer no reward, even had I the power to grant any. But there may be one, anyway, though granted not by me. I cannot compel you. I have searched your mind and found it clear and good.

"Now comes the choice. Will you help save the forest? Say no, and all of this will be like a dream, unremembered and lost, and you will be restored to the life of your people, recalling nothing.

"Say yes, and there will be fear and hardship, peril and strife. Reward there may be none. Consider well." There was silence and the Face stared at Alec out of the clouds and mist, still immobile, only the eyes alive and glowing.

As Alec considered, there came to his mind the picture of two animals, Scratch the raccoon and Stuffer the woodchuck, staring hopefully after him as he ran up the woodland path towards the house on that morning when they had first met. They really did need him, for something they could not do themselves. And if he did not help them, who would? His mind was made up at that moment.

"All right," he said. "I'm ready. Whatever it is, I'll try to do my best."

The great eyes seemed to soften for a second, and then the voice rang out.

"So—pity was the balance weight. It is seldom wrong to pity. I promise nothing, remember, but you may thank me yet. Now, there are things you must know if you are to act properly. When I have finished, the beasts will tell the rest so that you may do what must be done. Then comes the doing, and that is in your hands. Others may help before the end. Mowheen still lingers, the last of the three forest lords. If all comes to a right ending, perhaps we will speak again."

The voice took on a note of iron. "Look now upon your enemy, who threatens my Gate and must be defeated if the wood is to be saved."

The Face disappeared, and in its place in the swirling clouds, a circular shape began to form. It was like a round picture frame but with edges of living light. It grew larger and larger until it filled all the space before Alec's eyes.

A shape began to build in the center of the frame, a crouching, squat form. A naked, scaly tail was revealed and a narrow snout. Bright, black eyes stared directly at Alec as if he were clearly visible. The grayish-brown, dirty haunches tensed as the creature sat up and seemed to glare straight at the boy, malice and anger evident in its gaze.

It was an enormous rat.

4

Alec looked at the rat and the rat looked at Alec, or at least appeared to be looking at him. He could see that it was sitting on what seemed to be dark earth, but around it there was nothing but pearl gray light, with no background or any other detail to be seen.

As he looked more closely he could see that the animal was obviously the veteran of many fights. Its pointed snout was scarred by old wounds; and other white weals, long since healed, showed on its grizzled flanks and legs. As he watched, the rat sat up and wrinkled its nose, displaying big, sharp, yellow teeth and making its long whiskers twitch from side to side. Its large round ears were dirty and the left one had a triangular hole bitten out of one edge.

A friend of Alec's had owned a white rat, bought in a pet store, which had pink eyes and an engaging manner. Alec had held his friend's pet in his hand and the little creature had frisked about and played with his fingers, as tame and confiding as anything could be. But this rat he was watching was no pet, no playmate. From its bright and venomous black eyes came a scheming hatred and a concentrated malevolence. The very attitude of the beast was not animal-like at all, which puzzled the boy. He tried to think of what the difference might be, and it suddenly came to him.

It was confidence! The rat acted utterly confident, as if it were the absolute ruler of its world. There was an air of arrogance and triumphant vanity mixed with the hatred, the malice, and the cruelty. This creature believed itself to be the master of everything around it.

Why, thought Alec, not realizing what a terrible condemnation he was giving to his own birthright, it acted as if it were human! The thing's entire dirty body seemed to radiate a feeling of grim competence and ferocious command. Whatever he was involved in, the boy realized, he had an enemy whom he instinctively loathed, without knowing why, but whom he also feared.

Then the vision blurred and faded. All was mist and haze for a brief moment and then there was nothing and his mind went blank.

Alec was awakened by a feeling of pressure on his left arm. He opened his eyes and moved the arm, to realize he was lying on the grass. Looking straight up, he saw above him the night sky, full of blazing stars with the moon now directly overhead. He sat up. He was still in the circle of flat stones, it was still night, and beside him sat Scratch the raccoon, who had awakened him by pulling his arm.

"Are you all right?" said the raccoon.

Alec rubbed his head. He felt stiff, but otherwise fine. He looked around for the horde of animals that had ringed the enclosure. Where was the sea of eyes and bodies that had packed the little arena in the wood to overflowing? All were gone. No wait— not quite all. Besides Scratch, Stuffer the woodchuck was still there and a large skunk as well, who stared at Alec from a few feet away. Before he could get around to asking who the skunk was, a strange new voice said, "Good evening, young human. Look up if you want to see me." The voice felt hollow and echoing and soft, all at the same time.

Alec looked up and saw a large brown bird with a streaked breast, fluttering right over his head. As he stared, it came down, its wings beating soundlessly, and landed as lightly as one of its own feathers on the ground beside him. It was a big barred owl.

"My name's Soft Wing," he said to the boy. "We've watched you at night when you were asleep. Sometimes you snore."

"Never mind that," said Scratch impatiently. "We have to get him out of here and back to his house. Who cares if he snores?"

"Wait," said Alec. He reached out a hand and touched the owl's head, which felt as soft as down.

Obeying an urge to regain touch with the ordinary world again, he began to gently ruffle the feathers with the tip of one finger. The owl moved closer and his voice said, "That feels nice. Don't stop." His bird's mind voice was very different from the animals Alec had heard so far, being both quick and yet somehow floating or hovering as well as very gentle.

"Before we go anywhere," said the boy looking around at the others, "I have a lot of questions. And who is this?" he added, looking at the strange skunk.

"I'm Stamper," he began, but before he could say anything else, Scratch cut in again.

"We haven't got all night, Watcher," he said. "All of us here are the animals who are supposed to stay near you and help you. If some of us have to be away, then others of us can take over, so you'll always have a messenger or someone who can send word to the rest of us. Soft Wing can fly to your window at night and the rest of us can take turns being in the orchard or somewhere close by during the day. That's all there is to it."

"And I'm going to be with you all the time," said a small voice very near Alec's ear. Twisting his head, he saw Whisperfoot again balanced on his shoulder. She had run up his back without his even feeling it.

"There," she said in a satisfied tone. "Now someone with common sense, and not just a lot of silly quarrelsome males, can advise you."

"Will you really stay with me in the house?" said

Alec. He was delighted that she was back, and he had a feeling that she would be very useful in helping him to deal with the others.

Alec was still not altogether in touch with reality. He had just undergone an immensely disturbing experience and his mind was unsettled. At the back of all his thoughts was one major one: would he be able to measure up, to really do his part in whatever followed?

The gentle night wind stirred his hair and he shivered a little. Overhead, the moon was slowly passing from the zenith and the hour was obviously far advanced. There was no sign of light in the east, but the night was drawing on just the same. He turned to the skunk, who had been sitting patiently, waiting to be recognized.

"Hello, Stamper," said Alec. "Why did you pick that name?"

"Because he stamps his front feet before he—just before he—well, does what he does," said Scratch. A skunk's terrible weapon, the cloud of awful choking gas which he can release on demand, always makes other animals a little nervous. It is rather like having a time bomb around, or a giant firecracker which needs no fuse. Very few animals can bear the brunt of a skunk's attack, and because the gas is invisible, they find it all the more terrifying.

"I never use *it* unless I have to," said Stamper. His voice was calm and serene, and almost a little absentminded. "We skunks don't bother anyone much unless we're attacked. But the rats are different. At least these rats are. They aren't part of the woods and they hate all of us. They don't belong here and they want to kill or drive everything out, so there's no one but them left. They make us all feel sick somehow, because the way they think is wrong. *Twisted.*" He fell silent and Scratch took up the tale.

"We remembered something. Something about this place where we are now. The animals don't come here much, only the deer and they only eat the grass down low, like it is now, and then go away.

"But we remembered, a few of us, anyway, that this was a place we could come and ask for things. The humans, the red-skinned people that used to live here, came. Some even talked to the animals now and then. Not many of us remembered about this place but a few did."

"Were you one of them—one of the ones who remembered, I mean?" asked Alec.

"No," said the raccoon sadly. "I never heard about it; just that this was a good place to stay away from. Even the deer didn't really remember anything. They just felt they had to come and eat the grass here every so often."

"I remembered," said Stuffer unexpectedly. The big, fat woodchuck had been sitting quietly, not even nibbling the short grass of the circle. Alec had the feeling that the little clearing was indeed a special place if Stuffer could restrain his tremendous appetite for green things here.

The woodchuck continued. "Everyone thinks woodchucks sleep all winter. We sleep a lot, but we talk too. And we dream long, long dreams in the winter. My mother passed a dream on to me, seasons back when I was young. It was all about this place and what you could do here. You could talk here. *Something* here liked woodchucks and would help, if you needed it. I told Scratch about it."

"That's what I was going to ask next," said Alec. "Who did I talk to? He said he sent for me. What do you know about him anyway?"

He looked around, but there was no answer. The animals seemed embarrassed and confused. Only a blurred image of some need came from them to his mind, with the skunk seeming to be the one who felt it the most.

Finally Scratch spoke. "We don't know what you mean, Watcher," he said. " We were told to bring you here, but we didn't see anyone or anything. The *place* just told us, like when you know it's time to eat. It said, 'Go now and bring me a human. Do not be afraid. You can talk to some humans, you creatures who live near the Gate. Try a young one. They speak to us more clearly.' Then it said, 'Bring him here at night, all of you. Await my words.' We all, all the animals, felt it—the same way we know it's time to hunt, only stronger."

Alec realized then that his friends had no actual idea of the strange presence to whom he had spoken, no true understanding of what had happened. Their own experience was on a very different level and they were quite unable to grasp what he was asking. Manibozo was an instinct to them, although a very powerful one, rather than a person.

"Listen," he said, thinking hard. "First I've got to know more about rats—where they live, how they act—and especially, how this all started. What's going on here, anyway? Is there a war, or what?"

The raccoon again answered for the others. "The war hasn't really begun, not with real fighting, it hasn't. But it's only a matter of time. The brown rats have lived in the town dump of that human village near here for years, stealing from humans, destroying stored food, but never coming very far out of town. We don't have anything to do with them as a rule. If one comes out here into the real country—and once in a while one will—he doesn't last long. They almost always come at night."

"Not if I see them, they don't," said Soft Wing with a click of his curved beak. "Or Death Grip, my big cousin with the ears." All the animals flinched a little at this, even Stamper. The great horned owl, Soft Wing's cousin, feared absolutely nothing, not even the fearful smell of the skunk, and he was so strong and terrible that he was dreaded by the entire forest.

"Don't worry," said Soft Wing, noticing and rather enjoying the fright he had caused. "He'll be with us when he's needed. He's been observing the truce just like the rest of us."

"Anyway," continued Scratch, "the owls, and us too, killed any lone rats we ever saw outside the human village. Lately though, they have been coming out scouting in big gangs at night. Sometimes fifty or more, all fighters. That's too many for even the biggest of us to tackle alone. They weigh as much as five pounds apiece, and they aren't afraid to fight. Almost every night for the last two moons, they've sent at least one mob this size out of town, first on one side and then on the other."

"But why?" the boy asked. "Why don't they just stay in the dump?"

"We don't know," said Stamper. "Its one of the things we don't understand about them. But they want to move out and take over. We have too much evidence not to be sure what they plan to do. They talk to the other animals, brag a lot at times. It means just one thing: They plan to take over The Lot, the woods, everything!"

Stamper paused, then added, "They don't come from this land, you know. They're like the mice that already live in your house, coming from over the big water someplace. They've been here a while, but they won't ever *belong* here."

Alec looked at him with interest. The complete

menace in the news about the rats hadn't really sunk in yet, but he felt this handsome new ally had a clear way of putting things, even things hard to understand.

"Were you the skunk I heard yesterday?" said Alec. "I'm sorry, but I can't tell you apart, at least not yet."

"No, that was my uncle," said Stamper. "He's pretty old and slow, and when he finally realized you had heard him, he was already far away in the woods. He didn't like the idea of your hearing him at all, but he came and told me anyway. He knew we were all looking for a human who could talk, but it made him so nervous he went back to his hole and lay down. Probably still there. He's a bit old-fashioned. 'Talking humans,' he said. 'What next, talking trees?'"

"Never mind your uncle," broke in Scratch rudely. "Listen, Watcher, did you learn anything while you were lying down, or did you just dream, or what? Can you really help us? We all like you, you know, but still, there it is—we need help badly."

"I have to learn some more first, myself," said Alec. "How did you get to *me,* instead of someone else? What made you organize this truce? And I still don't see why a human is needed. All of you here, except Whisperfoot, could probably kill a lot of rats, all by yourselves."

"Yes, that's so," said Scratch. The big raccoon paused for a moment before speaking, as if trying to put his thoughts in order. "Look, we woods animals don't think the way the dump rats do. They all think together, move together, work together, and fight together. We just can't do that, not by ourselves. So we were told to try and get a human to help us. We have to have someone to keep us from arguing all the time, to *make* us be sensible and concentrate on the rats and not go off about our own private businesses. The truce in the wood is as far as we can go alone. Even at that, we have lots of trouble enforcing it. But we know we animals all have to stand together or the rats will smash us, because *they* stand together. Do you see?"

"I think so," said Alec. He saw indeed why the Spirit of the Wood needed another planner, a directing brain. The boy was still contemptuous of the rats, however, and felt the task a rather easy one. "Now look," he said, "I've got to get back home. When can I meet you all next, so we can talk?"

"Remember the bank of the stream where we gave you your talking lesson?" When Alec had said yes, Scratch went on. "Go upstream, to your left, and after a short walk you'll come to a clump of big fir trees, very close together. We'll be in the middle of that, waiting for you. When do you think you can come?"

"Wait a minute, wait a minute," said Soft Wing. "That's my roost, my place there. Why there?"

"Why do you think I picked that place?" the raccoon said. "You can't fly in the daylight—you're too blind; and this way you can meet with us and not have to move. Four other birds nest in that tree anyway. Who said you owned it?"

"That's fine," said Alec hastily, for Soft Wing was ruffling his feathers again and was obviously about to retort in a cutting manner. "I'll be there, I hope, by the middle of the afternoon, and I should have some good ideas by then. But now I have to get home."

Stuffer promptly got up and led the way out of the circle, into the clearing and up the path, with Scratch bringing up the rear. The skunk and the owl simply left. Animals do not usually say "Good-bye." Their lives are too uncertain and too subject to change to use the idea of leave-taking. If they are going to see you again, they will try to be at whatever meeting place they have arranged. No one is ever blamed for lateness. Who knows what may have kept him? Perhaps he narrowly escaped death only seconds before.

The stars were still bright enough to give light for the boy to pick his way from tree to tree of the old orchard. He finally reached the house, eased open the French doors of the library and slid inside. At this point the pinch of tiny claws on his earlobe told him that the deermouse was no happier to be inside the house than she had been before.

"Don't worry," he said silently. "There's no one around. I'll look after you."

"There is so someone around," she said. "That

stupid cat is asleep in a chair right over there. He may be half-witted but he still might try something if he saw me." Alec looked and saw that she was right. Worthless lay sprawled in an old spool chair near the fireplace, his eyes shut, his tail over his face. His even breathing was quite audible now that the outside door was shut.

Alec stole a look at the mantle clock. It said two minutes of three. He moved cautiously toward the door, one eye on the slumbering cat, and reaching the knob, slowly turned it. Only the tiniest scratching sound broke the silence of the big, dark room as the door slowly opened. Worthless lay immobile, all his feline faculties apparently useless. Alec slid through the narrow opening he had created and closed the door as silently as he had opened it.

Behind him in the library, two great yellow eyes stared at the door, blinked once, then opened again. A set of excellent claws, white and gleaming, were stretched from their owner's front paws, inspected and resheathed. The big cat wondered to himself if the young human had realized that the library door was not completely shut when he had gone out.

Worthless yawned smugly. This looked as if it would be an interesting summer after all.

5

The following day, Wednesday, dawned red and cloudy. The weather had changed in the small hours of the morning. A wind had risen from the east and rattled the shutters of the old house, warning of rain to come. It blew into Alec's open window and urged him into wakefulness at the usual seven o'clock time. He stirred sleepily and rolled over, one arm outflung on the pillow, dimly feeling that something needed doing.

He sat up staring out at the lowering clouds through the window. The gray light and the moan of the wind told him that the day would be a bad one. As the events of the past night came back to him, he shivered with remembered excitement. No one else in the whole world could say that they had a friend who was a raccoon, a woodchuck, an owl or—a mouse! Whisperfoot!

On reaching his bedroom the previous night, Alec had gone over it as carefully as he could in the dark, looking for a safe place for the deermouse to hide while he was out of the room, or even out of the house. He wanted a place that Worthless could not possibly reach, even if the bedroom door got left open through carelessness. The bureau and desk were ruled out. Lou Darden, who kept the house in a spotless condition, might open either to clean or simply inspect.

It was Whisperfoot herself who spotted a good place. Just above Alec's head, near one curled end of the big sleigh bed's headboard, a large knot some time in the past had popped out of the ancient pine paneling. The mouse had climbed up the bed and simply jumped in. Emerging a moment later, she had sneezed, but said the knothole joined an old and long-unused mouse residence further back in the wall, and aside from a little dust, it was perfectly clean.

Alec had gone to his bureau and taken one of his stock of seldom-utilized white hankerchiefs and torn a piece of it off. This he had pushed partway into the knothole, and the mouse had dragged it the rest of the way in. She reported that it made an excellent bed and that she was more than comfortable. Alec stuffed the torn handkerchief in his pants, to be discarded later. Then they had wished each other a good rest, and the boy had fallen asleep. . . .

Now here Whisperfoot was, calling cheerfully to him from her new nest.

"I'm right here, Watcher. Right where you put

93

me last night. And look what I found!" There was a brief scratching sound. "Come on out, you! I told you it was perfectly safe. For the tenth time, he won't eat you."

Alec realized that Whisperfoot was not talking to him but to someone else, and waited expectantly, his eyes fixed on the knothole. The pretty deermouse emerged first, jumped down from the top of the headboard and sat looking up at the hole.

"Come on," she urged again. "I'm right here sitting next to the human. He doesn't bite."

Out of the hole peered a small, brown, whiskered face with two round ears. Slowly there followed a fat little body and a longish tail, though still much shorter than Whisperfoot's. Finally a plump, rather scruffy-looking house mouse emerged and sat blinking nervously at the mouth of the hole.

"I thought you said last night—" began Alec to Whisperfoot, but she cut him off before he could bring up her previously expressed low opinion of house mice.

"Never mind that," she said quickly. "He's not a bad sort and he wants to be helpful. They all do, as a matter of fact, all of his people, and I think we can use them."

"Here, you," she continued to the other mouse, who seemed frightened out of his wits. "Tell the human your new name, the one I gave you, and tell him what you told me earlier."

Alec waited as patiently as he could while the house mouse twitched his whiskers and blinked and stared. Finally the boy was about to speak himself, when a small scared voice in his mind formed a picture of the mouse skulking and creeping about the edge of a wall, flattened to the floor so tightly that he was practically moving on his stomach.

"I see," said Alec, trying not to laugh. "You called him Creeper, I guess?"

"Creeper will do," said Whisperfoot. "There, Creeper, aren't you proud? You have a real, human name. Don't you feel braver already?"

"No," said the house mouse timidly. "I don't. But I don't think I ever will. I never heard of a brave house mouse. It's all very well for you woods people to talk," he went on with a sudden rash of speech. "I'd like to see you living with a cat as a permanent member of the household, mousetraps everywhere, stuff left all over that tastes like good food and kills you dead, humans pouring boiling water down your hole whenever they see you, and all that!"

"Why don't you go live in a hole in a tree?" said Whisperfoot, cleaning her immaculate whiskers as she spoke. "I'll help you find a nice place." There was a twinkle of delicate humor in her mind voice, but although Alec caught it, Creeper was too appalled to notice.

"Live in the woods! In a tree!" The house mouse's horror and indignation were so strong he actually squeaked out loud. "Out in the open, in a place full of owls and weasels and minks and foxes and skunks and hawks—and—" he sputtered for a moment and then went on. "And be cold and wet all winter and be flooded in the spring and afraid to go out in the summer and hungry in the fall?" His whole fat body shook at the very idea.

"Too bad," said Whisperfoot, supressing a ladylike yawn. "I had such a nice hole in mind. You could have shared it with two pine mice. It's built in the bottom of a crow's nest." The teasing note in her voice was very apparent to Alec, but not to the house mouse.

The boy had enjoyed watching the deermouse poking fun at the fat, absurd, little creature, but he now decided enough was enough.

He said soothingly to Creeper, "I'm sure no one will make you go and live outside. Not if you don't want to. And you can always come up here. I'll keep the door shut and see there are no mousetraps left around the room. Maybe I can find some cheese now and then. How's that?"

"Very handsome, if and when, and no offense meant," said Creeper. "Smelling is believing, as the saying goes. Not but what I'm sure anyone this lady says is a friend, really is. It's just that talking to a human is something new to me. Usually at the other end of a broom or jumping on chairs yelling, that's the way we see them—we house mice, I mean." He seemed more relaxed at the boy's words, however, and settled back on his fat rump, eyeing them both, his beady eyes no longer so furtive and wary.

"Now, Whisperfoot," said Alec. "What did you mean when you said Creeper and the other house mice could be useful? How are they of any use to us when they never leave this house?"

"He found me asleep this moring, early," said the deermouse. "He was checking the old knothole because no one has used this room for a long time and he thought you might have left some food around he could steal when no one was looking. I woke up and asked him what he wanted, and he almost ran away, he was so frightened."

"Now then," interrupted Creeper. "Not so much of this frightened business. Careful is the word for it, if you please." He was obviously recovering his nerve and was now quite cocky.

"We got to talking about this and that," resumed the deermouse, "both of us being small, and I told him about you and what we were trying to do out in the wood. He got terribly excited, because he says the other house mice know something about this rat business. He went running off before I could stop him and said he'd be back as quickly as he could. I could see you were still asleep and it wasn't dawn yet, so I just waited for him. He came back a little before you woke up and told me he'd been talking to his friends. But I think he'd better tell you himself."

Alec could see that the dainty deermouse didn't want to admit that she found that the two kinds of mice had a great deal in common—much more, for instance, than perhaps either might with larger animals.

"I'd be glad to hear what he has to say," said Alec. "What is it you know, Creeper?"

The dingy little animal swelled with importance at the question, until he looked like a midget fur balloon with attached ears and whiskers.

"We know a good deal, we house mice." He preened his whiskers with an air of mystery. "We have our own ways of getting news. We have friends and relatives living in lots of places, even in town where all the houses are. Never been there myself. Too far to go, in my opinion, for a busy mouse with affairs of his own. Why, I have to help find food for a whole family and let me tell you, it takes some—"

"Yes, I'm sure it does," said Alec impatiently. "But we want to know about the rats. What do you know about them, and how do you know it?"

Eventually, with both Whisperfoot and the boy prodding him and dragging him away from his own troubles every so often, this was how his story came out:

"Us house mice are just as disturbed about dump rats coming here as any of you woods animals. Brown rats kill us house mice when they can find us. They even go hunting for us when they are feeling mean.

We have no way to resist, because we're so much littler. Nothing but the size of our holes and our quickness saves us. But rats are pretty quick, too. Making a small hole bigger is a much easier job than chewing a new one, you know. They even eat us, and they like our little babies."

It seemed that Creeper and his friends and relatives were in constant communication with all the other house mice who lived in nearby houses, and these in turn with still others, closer to Mill Run, and these finally with mice who actually lived in the town itself. Despite their fear of the outside world, house mice do go out on occasion, usually at night, to pay visits and look for new homes. This is when they meet and exchange news.

And now, the town mice of Mill Run had some recent news. A certain few of them were actually allowed to live near the village dump by the rats, and were not molested. Occasionally the rats even gave them food. In exchange, the mice were expected to furnish the rats with any news they might have of happenings of interest in and around the town. It was they who had passed on the recent information about the rats.

For some time now, the rats had been asking their mouse informants everything they could think of about all the country surrounding Mill Run village. Recently, however, their questions had been only about one area, The Lot. The mice had told them

99

as little as possible, pleading ignorance about a place so far away and wild, but they hastened to pass on the question and its meaning to their cousins in the country. "Look out," they had said, "we think the rats might be coming your way."

This was Creeper's information. "When considered," said Alec to Whisperfoot, "it tells us pretty much what we already knew, that the dump rats are planning some kind of attack."

But then something else occurred to him. He and the local animals had to know much, much more about the plans of the rats. And the house mice might help.

He quickly shared the thought with the two mice.

"Look," he said to Creeper, "you house mice don't want rats out here any more than the woods animals or us humans do. So you'll have to help. Can you arrange to have news of what the rats are doing brought every night from one house mouse to another, until it gets to me?"

Creeper looked dubious for a moment, and scratched one ear while he thought. "We don't go out every night, you know, not right outside. Very dangerous, that is, and not done often."

"Well, it will just have to be done," said Alec sternly. "You have just as much of an interest in keeping those rats out of here as we do. Besides," he added, "you could take turns, couldn't you? There must be a lot of you."

"I don't know," said Creeper. "It will have to be thought about. I'll have to talk to the others. Us house mice aren't much for wars and danger and things like that. The others may not like the idea. But I'll talk to them."

"Be sure you do," said the deermouse, bristling with indignation. "If the rats come to The Lot, what do you think will happen to you?" But Creeper had already vanished into the knothole and was gone.

"You really let him have it," said Alec admiringly to his small ally. "Do you think he'll try to help?"

"I can't be sure," said Whisperfoot. "They're not a bad sort, these little dirty things, but what cowards they are! One of my own people, or even a meadow mouse, would be worth fifty of them. House mice never stop thinking about hiding for a minute!"

"Just a moment," said Alec. "You've given me an idea! Why couldn't we get the house mice in the dump to pass information to the meadow mice? I saw some in the Council Glade the other night."

"Why, that would probably work quite well," said Whisperfoot, sitting up on the bedstead. "I'll go and talk to them about it right now." She darted over to the open window and shot down the vine out of sight before Alec could say another word.

He dressed himself, remembering to tie his shoes, and went down the front stairs to breakfast. His grandfather was not yet up, and so he went into the kitchen, where he found Lou washing dishes.

"Just a second, honey, and I'll get you some breakfast," she said. "You'll look a little less bouncy than yesterday. Weather got you down?"

"No," said Alec, thinking quickly. "It just seems like a sleepy sort of a day, that's all." He looked out at the cloudy sky and the wind-tossed trees, visible through the kitchen window. "It's going to rain, isn't it?"

"Yep," she answered, "sure is, from the look of things. A northeast wind does bring rain at this season. Maybe you can stay in today and watch TV instead of going outside and getting all wet. Darden has to go to town for supplies in a little while now. Like to ride in with him?" As she spoke, she had been moving about the kitchen, and in no time at all, cereal, milk, and orange juice were planked down on the kitchen table.

Alec nodded as he began to eat. "Yes, I would like to go," he said. "I've never had a really good look at Mill Run."

"Not so much of a town," said Lou. "Still, I was born there so I expect I favor it. It is pretty in summer and not so cluttered as some, nor so full of tourists and nasty little stores and such, either. Soon as they get rid of that dirty town dump, the way they're fixing to this year, the place will look real nice, the way it did when I was a girl. I just hope that new shopping center the village selectmen voted for ain't going to be ugly, and— Land's sakes, what's the matter, boy?"

Alec had suddenly choked on his milk and his face had turned bright red. Of course! That was why the rats had to move! That was why they were scouting The Lot. They wanted to make it their new home.

Lou pounded Alec's back and mopped the milk off his face with her apron.

"Now pay attention to what you're doing, Alec. Finish your breakfast and I'll give a yell for Darden. Your grandpa felt tired this morning, I guess. He works too hard on his books for an old man, if you want my opinion. Seems as if no one in this world will ever do what's good for them. I'll take the Professor his breakfast up on a tray. That riles him worse than anything I know. He'll get up so fast you won't even see him go, he gets that angry when I pretend I think he's ailing." She winked at Alec and made him laugh.

As Lou bustled about the kitchen, the boy looked out at the gray sky, now even more ill-omened than when he had awakened. As he watched, the first patter of rain sounded on the roof and big drops began to hit the window panes. It soon settled down to a steady, hard downpour, and the muffled roar of water pouring off the tin rainspouts and the high peaked roofs maintained itself as a constant noise in the background.

Alec drank the last of his milk, his thoughts gloomy. Would the animals still expect him to come out to the woods this afternoon, in this weather? He decided, on consideration, that they probably would. Rain almost certainly didn't mean much to wild animals. They probably figured that he was capable of getting out in any weather, so long as it was daytime. He owned a yellow slicker, a matching rain hat and boots, all of which had been carefully packed by his mother and were now upstairs. Why shouldn't he use them? He decided to try a test shot.

"There's no reason for Grandpa not to let me out in the rain so long as I have my rain things on, is there, Lou?" he asked innocently.

Lou cocked a wise blue eye at him. "Grandpa, nothing, Mr. Smarty. It's me that says who goes out and in what. Why, Professor March probably wouldn't take notice if you ran out in your bare skin! I see what you're about, trying to get around me like that!" She considered, still looking at him, then glanced outside at the weather.

"It's still coming down pretty hard. Go to town with Darden and maybe it will let up some. If you still want to go out later, we'll see."

"Okay," said Alec. He knew when he had won a partial victory and decided not to push his luck.

"I'll go get my stuff and then look for John. Thanks for breakfast."

"You do that. Have a good time in town, now, and don't let Darden get into trouble." Alec couldn't imagine John getting into trouble, and decided the last comment was not meant to be serious.

Alec put on his rain gear and went outside to see his turtle. He felt that he had neglected the poor animal and wished he had thought of him earlier. But who could think of a pet turtle with all the other things that had happened?

The box turtle seemed delighted with the rain, which had brightened his black and yellow shell. While Alec watched from a perch on the rail of the back porch, the turtle dug up and ate several large earthworms from the dirt floor of his pen. John was not in sight and Alec had a sudden thought. Could turtles talk? He directed his thoughts as hard as he could, but there was no response at all. Then he tried "listening" with his mind, to see if the beast could or would send him any message in return. To his amazement, he did pick up a dim mental picture. Not surprisingly, however, it contained only a blurred view of earthworms, lots and lots of earthworms, and a feeling of hunger as well. Alec tried again to send a message of his own, even thinking of himself digging earthworms and giving them to the turtle. But no sensible answer came back, only the dim thoughts of food and appetite. Discouraged, he decided turtles were simply not "tuned in," at least not to him.

He got up from the rail and went around the corner of the house. John had pulled the car out of the barn and was just getting in when Alec appeared.

"John, Lou said you were going to town and I could come," he said as he climbed into the car.

"I was only ready this second. Glad you could make it," said John amiably. His sole concession to the weather was a battered hunter's cap of leather and a thin denim jacket which matched his blue pants. On looking around, Alec saw that several flats of flowers, young plants and bunches of cut flowers, were carefully arranged on the back seats, and with them were some bags of new asparagus and boxes of strawberries.

"I'm a deacon over to our Congregational church in town," said John, seeing his glance. "There's some old and sick folks as don't get out much and I bring them a little garden sass and plants and flowers now and again. Cheers them up, to eat fresh-growed food and see things coming up as if they was growing outside. Your grandpa don't mind, 'cause he knows I grow enough for us and them, too. As a matter of fact, your grandma, Mrs. March, done the same when she was alive, poor lady. So it's kind of a house custom, you might say."

Alec was interested and asked what a deacon was, as the big station wagon rolled down the long driveway under the dripping trees. They chatted about this and other matters until the town's central green, with its bronze Minuteman, was reached. The whole drive had only taken a few minutes, and Alec was surprised to find out how close Mill Run village actually was to The Lot.

They bought groceries from a long list provided

by Lou and then went calling. Most of the people they visited were elderly, except for one younger woman surrounded by swarms of rather tattered-looking children. One old lady gave Alec a sugar cookie and told him that he looked exactly like his father. She also told him that his grandmother was still remembered and missed. "She was a real saint," said the old lady, adding in typical New England fashion, something which was quite lost on Alec, "in spite of being Episcopal."

Finally, all had been visited and John said they could now go home. Light rain was still coming down but the sun seemed to be trying to get through high above.

As John started the car, Alec said, "John, Lou said there was a town dump they were going to turn into a shopping center or something. Could I see it? I've never seen a real dump before."

"Kids always want to see something nobody ever thought of asking about," said John, eyeing him aslant. "Now what in tarnation do you want to see the town disgrace for? We've been trying to get the selectmen to vote that mess out of here for ten years now and you act like it was a national monument."

"Well," said Alec, "maybe there won't be any when I grow up. Maybe they'll all be extinct. Then I'll never see one. Couldn't we, anyway?"

"So be it, if you really want to," said John, shaking his head. "Mightn't be a bad idea at that. If you ever get to be president, you can keep all the dumps in the country from getting out of hand."

They drove a short distance down a pleasant tree-shaded lane, and turned a sharp corner onto another road, which brought them to a dirt track running away from town. A little way down, beyond a small signpost, lay the village dump, and the smell of it caught Alec's nose even before it came into sight. On reaching the edge of it, they parked.

It was an ugly sight, even softened by the rain, but also fascinating to Alec. A swollen mound of debris bulging out to about the area of an acre or more, it was built up of garbage, rotten automobile tires and rusty tin cans. Small fires smoked here and there, spitting out greasy, gray smoke as the raindrops hit them. Parts and bodies of old, abandoned cars lay about in various places at the edge. The whole scene was inexpressibly sad and disgusting, especially after the lovely country town with its neat gardens, green lawns, and white houses.

Nevertheless, it was not without interest. Abandoned toys lay here and there. Alec noticed a broken tricycle, some tot's abandoned vehicle, and near it a headless doll. A refuse heap of human civilization, like those of the ancient past, it accurately reflected the lives of the people who had thrown their unwanted and used-up belongings here.

And somewhere near it or under it lay the stronghold of the rats! A more evil-appearing castle or fortress would be hard to imagine, the boy reflected.

Looking over his shoulder, Alec could see the church steeple and realized that the town was really quite close.

"That's right," said John, seeing his look. "People are just plain lazy. They been using this place since the whole town only had ten people in it and the town's grown out right to the dump now. Even so, we had to get up a petition before them stubborn selectmen would do anything."

"Aren't they going to build something here, some new buildings, Lou said?"

"Yep," said John. "Nothing so nice as a park, but better than this anyway. Trees don't pay taxes, and that's all them selectmen can think about, more taxes. They're going to bury all this muck by bull-dozing it into that hollow over there. That'll fill in an old cave full of garbage and vermin that's supposed to be hidden just down the slope. They'll level that little hill next and then they can take dirt and spread it over the whole area and make a foundation. On top of that goes a new gas station, cleaning estab-lishment and drugstore, all in nice, new, shiny, con-crete buildings. Personally, I'd rather have trees, but when I made the suggestion, Old Caleb Wilson looked at me like I was crazy. Still, it'll be better than this mess, full of filth and rats. Some of the boys has come out here at night and plinked at the rats with their .22 rifles. Don't get many, though. The rats learned to lay low after a little of that. Rats is smart."

"Why don't they come and kill all the rats with guns?" said Alec. "Or maybe poison them?"

"Well, you're sure in a bloodthirsty mood," said John. "Sonny, even if the whole town come out here, they'd maybe shoot three rats between them. Them rat holes are all over this dirty mess and all through the hill and the hollow beyond. You might get a lot with poison gas pumped in the holes, the way I hear tell they do on ships, but there's so many holes that most of the rats would get away anyhow. Poisoning 'em would cost a fortune.

"No, the best way to get rid of rats is to get rid of the dump. A few will always be around. Nobody ever figured out how to get rid of all the rats in creation. But most of them will light out and go somewhere else."

The boy felt suddenly cold. Indeed, the rats would go somewhere else. And he had a good idea where, even if John did not! Somehow, in some arcane manner, the rats had learned or guessed what was going to happen to the dump. And they must have taken very careful steps to locate new territory in which to settle.

"Well, you seen all you want?" asked John, switching on the engine. "You can say you saw the worst little town dump in all the whole Nutmeg State. That makes you an expert on dumps." The car turned and they headed back.

110

Alec saw that he was expected to smile, but his heart wasn't in it. The fact that adult humans, with rifles and even poison gas, were so pessimistic about their ability to destroy rats discouraged him greatly. What on earth could one boy and a lot of woods animals do if grownups were unable to do much? He thought for a moment of enlisting John in the cause, but it was only a passing thought. It would be easy to give up all responsibility, stop worrying, let a grown-up take over. But as soon as the thought appeared, Alec dismissed it. The trust had been laid upon *him*. If an adult could have done the job, one would have been selected. He would just have to work it out himself. He sighed as he thought of all the problems. He had to learn so much more so quickly.

The rain was now only a mist, and the sun had actually come through in places and lit the black, glistening asphalt ahead of them and the trees on either side. As the big car approached the stretch of road leading to The Lot, Alec watched the sides of the road carefully. The station wagon was cruising along a section of state forest which lay directly between The Lot and the Mill Run dump, and it had occurred to the boy that he had better start learning how the land lay. He wondered if the rats, when they came, would be smart enough to circle The Lot and come from the west or south, rather than come directly from the east.

As the car rolled up the long drive, Alec sat

silent, thinking of battles and what he knew about them. In early school grades, he had learned about Paul Revere, the battle of Bunker Hill, "Don't fire until you see the whites of their eyes," and such matters as that. From the conversation of his parents and other adults, he had picked up bits and pieces about World War II and the other later wars that plagued the world. But it didn't help much. The rats didn't wear red coats like the old British used to, there were no guns (or anyone to shoot them) and no planes, ships, helicopters or atom bombs, either. It was all very discouraging. How could he find out more about real battles and how they were fought?

Then he suddenly thought of his grandfather. Professor March knew almost everything in the world, reflected Alec. Perhaps he could be asked for help in such a way that he would have no idea what the reason behind the questioning was.

The station wagon came to a stop in front of the house, abruptly jolting him out of his reflections.

"Hope you liked your ride," said John. "You seemed pretty quiet on the way back. That dump get you down a bit, maybe?" he asked shrewdly.

"Yes, it did," said Alec hastily. "It seemed awfully dark and gloomy and full of lost, broken things. But I really enjoyed myself. Thanks a lot for the ride."

"Any time," said John, reflecting to himself that the boy was a deep one.

Meanwhile, Alec had run up the two front

steps and gone in the door. The idea of getting hold of his grandfather at once had seized him, and he was determined to extract as much information as he could immediately. The rain had entirely stopped. The wind had died and sunlight sparkled on drops of water gleaming on every bush, tree and blade of grass.

He found the Professor in the library as expected, working at his cluttered desk. The old man was delighted to see him.

"I understand you have made your first trip into town," he observed, looking at his young grandson with affection. "Hardly a roaring metropolis like New York, but infinitely more restful. Fresh air, too. What did you see—anything interesting?"

"Oh, lots of things," said Alec vaguely. "Nothing special. That's not why I came in here, though. Grandpa, I've been thinking about what you said last night, all about King Richard and the way people fought battles in the Middle Ages, and all that. And I got interested because I wondered what people did when they didn't even have swords and spears and battle-axes and things. How did they fight then? Can you fight well if you don't even know how to hit people with a sword or even a stick? Did the ancient people fight battles without any of those things? Do you have to have swords at least before you can have a war?"

The Professor was very pleased, both with his

grandchild and also, truth to tell, with himself. The old man had been afraid that it would be boring for a youngster to listen all summer to someone of his advanced age. The Professor beamed. Alec saw that he had pleased him somehow, and felt better about his hope of getting some useful information.

"Now then, Alec, you want to know whether people fought organized wars before the invention of tools and weapons. Do I understand you clearly?"

"That's right," said the boy. "How did they fight? What did they do if they wanted something other people had and hadn't any spears or knives or anything to fight them with?"

"Well, my boy, this is rather hard to say. You see, there aren't any people in the world today who are so primitive that they have no weapons. The Australian aborigines are pretty far down the cultural scale. But even they have spears, and they invented boomerangs, those curved things that come back when you throw them. The South African Bushmen use bows and poisoned arrows, and they, too, are very primitive.

"Going back into the remote past, the cave men —the Neanderthalers and the Magdalenian people called Cro-Magnons—they all used weapons, beautifully-made ones at that. Even the so-called apemen used sticks and bones and stone tools, mostly crude hand axes. So you see, if even the most primitive humans had weapons, your question becomes almost impossible to answer. Weapons and humans seem to go together, unfortunately, and always have."

Alec reflected. He was sure that his grandfather had some vital information, if he could only think of the right way to ask him. There just had to be some way of getting it. Something the old man had just said came back to him.

"Grandpa, you said the apemen had tools. But how about the apes themselves? Do gorillas have sticks and things out in the jungle where they live, to fight with? I've seen them at the Bronx Zoo, but all they had was a ball and an old car tire."

"Well, if you must leave the human level, there are some analogies, I suppose," said Professor March, in an interested voice. "Gorillas have no tools, although I have read recently that some chimpanzees do use sticks to extract white ants from their nests for food. And neither chimpanzees nor gorillas fight wars. They are, fortunately for their own souls, not 'intelligent' enough, if that is the right word." He looked away, over Alec's head and stared blankly at the bookcase, obviously thinking.

"Baboons *do* fight in packs though. They have regular territories, just like countries only much smaller than ours, of course, and they defend these from other baboons. Some of the reports, I believe, speak of hundreds of them, real armies, having pitched battles. Is that what you wanted to know?" he asked the boy.

"Well, I guess so," said Alec. "Actually, I mean, what I want to know is *how* they fight. Do they send out scouts, and well, set traps for each other? Stuff like that?"

"I'm afraid my memory's not too strong on the intimate details of baboon military campaigns," chuckled Professor March. "I guess they probably do something of the sort. They are rather intelligent brutes, and a great nuisance to farmers in Africa, if my recollections serve." He paused and looked sharply at the boy. "What are you really after, Alec? This seems to be very important to you. You haven't smiled once since you came in here."

Alec shifted nervously and scuffed one sneaker on the faded oriental rug. He could not meet his grandfather's piercing eye.

"It's just, well, I got to know about war, that's all! I thought you could tell me how two sides fight a war, and it would be simpler if I left out all the weapons and guns and things, so I could understand what—what a general does, or somebody that tells soldiers what to do and where to go." He looked anxiously up at the white head above him. "That's all, honest."

The Professor sat back, satisfied. "I see now," he said. "What you want to know are the *principles* of war. And of course you didn't know how to ask, so you did it this way. Not a bad way, either. Do you know for a moment I had a crazy mental picture of an army of animals marching in ranks!" Fortunately for Alec, this last observation was made while Dr. March was lighting his pipe, so he could not see his grandson's face.

"The actual principles, the basic ideas which govern any war, are very old indeed. And very simple, too, at least to talk about or describe. It's putting them into practice that's the hard part. Most of them were written down by the Chinese two thousand years before Christ.

"One very successful American general, named Forrest, who had no formal military training but who learned all by himself exactly what to do, once said that success in battle meant 'fustest with the mostest.' What he meant was, get to a key position with more men than the enemy has in the same place. Somebody else, I forget just who, said, 'Hit 'em where they ain't!' He meant that the place to strike hard was where the enemy least expected you. If the enemy was watching and guarding the north end of some valley, say, then you should attack the south end.

"Other successful military men have said other things. Napoleon said that the pursuit of a beaten enemy must be instantaneous and pressing. He said that if a beaten army were followed, constantly attacked and harassed by cavalry or light troops and given no chance to recover, it would then be totally destroyed and never able to re-form and fight again.

Is this the sort of thing you wanted to know?"

Alec's brown eyes were shining. "Yes, that's it! That's just what I need. Do you know more? What happens when an army is coming and you know pretty well where, but not when? How do you fight them if you have less soldiers than they do?"

Smiling at Alec's enthusiasm, Professor March continued. "It seems to me that if you knew where the enemy was coming at you, half the problem would be solved. You could pick the place you wanted to fight. For instance, suppose there was a narrow place, like a mountain pass, that he had to come through. You could block it in front and attack from both sides."

"But how?" asked the boy.

"Look, Alec. I've told you the basis. It's simple really. There almost always is a defensible obstacle. If not a mountain pass, then a swamp or a wide river. If the ground is in the enemy's favor, perhaps flat with no obstacles or defenses, why then you re-treat or advance, go back or forward, to a place where there *are* obstacles and defenses. If the enemy knows what you're doing, you have to be careful. If not, it's pretty easy."

"I get it," said Alec thoughtfully. "You wait until the enemy *comes to you,* where you're waiting for them, in the best place to fight."

"Exactly," said Professor March, blowing a large smoke ring.

118

"But how do you do that?" said Alec, puzzled. "I don't see what you can do to make them come just one way and not others, unless they just happen to, by mistake or something."

"I'll tell you," said his grandfather, "and you'll see how easy it is, or rather, how easy it looks. If the enemy is smart, it may not be so easy to do! Still, suppose an enemy army is marching on your country. You want them to come only one way, and no other. So you could start rumors. You let them know that the other ways are guarded. You move men around to all the other places and make them look as strong as possible. And you make the one special place look weak. You keep the men you have there hidden and any defenses concealed. Then you hope. Often, it works. If it doesn't, you must wait until they actually begin to march. Then you attack continuously, but with only a few men, called skirmishers or scouts. You may add more men to them if you can and if it's needed or called for. You try to make any other route so unappealing and difficult that the enemy will half drift, half be driven, into the one way you want. How's that?"

"Great! That's wonderful! But what about time, Grandpa? Suppose you're not sure when the enemy will come? What do you do then?"

"That's difficult," said Professor March. "You could get into trouble. But there are people in every army called intelligence officers. They are the ones who try to find out what the enemy will do. Now, your intelligence men will do their best to find out how and when the enemy will move. And each army gets news from spies, too, people who live in the enemy country and pretend to be part of the enemy. Sometimes they help a lot; sometimes their news is too late or wrong. But I suppose that's not what you wanted. You just want the beginning principles, eh?"

"No," said Alec. "I mean, yes. I mean, that's great, just what I wanted. Thanks a million, Grandpa, for all that stuff. I really understand now, I think. Well, I got to go." He ran for the door. Just as he got there, however, another thought sprang into his mind. From somewhere, the strange word, the mysterious name of the "other helper" flashed across his mind. He stopped and came slowly back to the desk, where his grandfather still sat looking at him.

"Forget something, son?" Professor March said to him.

"I saw a funny word the other day," said Alec, choosing his words carefully. "It was written in a book, I guess, but I don't remember. Maybe I heard it. It was Mowheen. Do you know who it is?"

"Mowheen," mused his grandfather. "No, doesn't ring a bell. Wait, though, I do remember something, but very dimly. It's an Indian word, by gum. What the devil does it mean? I heard it years ago, or read it. Alec, you ought to take up my profession. You ask the darndest questions and they're hard to answer."

The boy waited silently.

"Mowheen, Mowheen. Algonquin, maybe?" The old man ruminated, chewing on his short mustache with his lower lip and teeth. Then he stared out of the open window at the sunlit lawn in front of the house.

"Got it," he said suddenly. "The old boy's not senile, not yet, he's not! Now, I wonder—where did you see that word?"

"I can't remember, Grandpa. Who is it? Is it a man?"

The Professor shook his head. "No, son. Not a man. Mowheen is the old Indian name for the great black bear."

6

Alec picked his way cautiously over boulders and rotting logs, through wet laurel bushes and clumps of fern. Indian pipes poked through the leafmold, skunk cabbage spread all around, and beautiful scarlet-and-tan mushrooms showed here and there in shadowed nooks. The birds called all about them, and he could hear crows cawing in the distance. To his right, the brook, swollen from the recent rain, babbled and gurgled as it raced through tussocks and around great rocks, straining to reach the distant pond in the marsh.

He soon saw the clump of seven big firs ahead, so dark that they made a menacing blot in the sunlit forest. They were huge old trees and their needles were so dense that he could see nothing through them, even when he had drawn quite close. Other eyes, looking out, could see better, however, assisted by keen ears and noses.

"We all got here, Watcher," came the now familiar voice of Scratch, "and you're even earlier than we hoped. Do you have any ideas? We're under this first tree."

Alec got to his knees without answering and crawled under the prickly outer branches. The ground, although completely dry, was rather prickly, too, with all the twigs, needles and cones which had fallen. Inside it was just like being in a tent. When his eyes grew adjusted to the dim light, he could see the black mask of the big raccoon, the grizzled head of the woodchuck and the black-and-white skunk, all sitting at the base of the tree waiting for him. On a low branch, about three feet above the carpet of needles, sat Soft Wing.

"Get your breath back, Watcher," said the big raccoon. "We were worried that they wouldn't let you out if it was raining. I've noticed that humans don't like to get rained on."

"I was worried, too," said Alec. "The rain stopped though, so there was no trouble. But Whisperfoot arranged about the messengers to come from town, not me. Whisperfoot, you tell them, because you did it all."

"I did some work, but Watcher thought of it all, really," she said, jumping from his body to a low branch nearby. There she began to groom herself, continuing to talk. "I went to see the meadow mice. It's working out fine, at least so far. They have sent out messengers to contact the house mice and other meadow mice all the way into town. By tonight, we'll

123

have a chain of mice passing news back and forth regularly."

The pretty deermouse tried to give the credit to Alec, of whom she had come to be very fond, but she didn't really mind being the center of attention. She asked the other animals to pass the word that no house mouse was to be molested or killed if it was seen out of doors. This was necessary, because house mice had not been included in the truce the forest animals had arranged.

"I'll do my best," said Scratch. "Some of the bad elements aren't going to like it, but they'll just have to agree. I have a complaint about one of the meat-eaters chasing one of our local rabbits. I finally found him and gave him a real going over, but you can't trust any of them except Slider and his family. They're good people and with us all the way, but the others, well, you have to keep bearing down on them." His mind had formed a sort of mass picture of a whole jumble of different animals and Alec couldn't understand what the raccoon was talking about.

"What do you mean," he said. "Are some animals not being peaceful around here? Who's Slider, any-way?"

"Here he is, coming up the stream right now," said Stamper the skunk. "He wanted to meet you, but he and his family were fishing miles away until today and he couldn't get back in time for last night. Shake yourself off outside, will you? I don't want to get soaked." This last was addressed not to Alec but to someone else.

A long, brown, slick-furred body wormed into the tent made by the tree and sat up on short hind legs, balancing on a long, heavy tail. A bluntly-pointed head with small, sleek ears and large, brown eyes faced the boy at his own eye level. It was a big dog otter.

"Hello there, Watcher. Glad to see you." The mind voice was almost noisy, quite hearty and rolling, and it told quite as much about the animal talking as the quiet tone of the skunk or the argumentative, gravelly impression given by the raccoon.

"Sorry I missed the meeting the other night," said Slider. "You know how it is, had to go check out a trout farm over to the east a few miles. Sure enough, the netting was loose. The humans will be plenty annoyed when they look at some of the tanks. Still, I have seven to feed, counting myself. What's going on here? Anything been decided yet?" His whole manner was confident, breezy, and yet extremely alert. Alec decided on the spot that this was a very valuable ally.

"We were about to tell Watcher about all the bad elements, the hold-outs, when you arrived," said Scratch. "Since most of them are relatives of yours, why don't you take over?" Here again was a sample of animal politeness. If anything rude had to be said,

125

it ought to be kept in the family, so to speak, and not said by other, unrelated animals.

"Right," said Slider. He inched closer to the fascinated boy, who could now detect a distinct odor of fish about him, not really too unpleasant but still noticeable.

"The fact is," said the otter, "some of my smaller relatives are just not easy to keep in line. No sense of humor, no responsibility, no team spirit. Fill your own belly and never mind tomorrow, or anyone else either. Can't think ahead. I'll show you some of them."

Into Alec's mind came the picture of a small, brown animal with white underparts. It was long and slim and darted around the ground on tiny legs, bending like a furry snake to get around obstacles. He recognized it as a weasel. Before he could say so, another animal projection appeared, this time of a larger beast, so dark brown as to be almost black, but shaped very similarly. The boy had no trouble with this one either, identifying it as a mink, a fact made even more evident because it was shown swimming gracefully in the picture. Then came still another picture of a large brownish spotted cat with tufted ears and a short, stub tail, bounding through the forest on big furry pads.

"That last one, he's no relative of mine," added the otter, interrupting the pictures. "Fortunately, he's the only one of his kind around and we told him to plain get out, and come back in a moon or so, or we'd all get after him, all of us at once. He's a big coward and he left, spitting and snarling. He knew we meant it, though. I don't think he'll be back for awhile."

Alec had recognized the bobcat by this time, and he asked if there were any more animals still to come.

"That's about it," said Slider. "Wait, there's another, or I should say, others. They're the worst killers of the whole bunch because there are so many of them. There's probably one around now, out under the leaves. Wait here a bit, I'll see if I can find a sample."

With a graceful, looping motion, like a giant brown inchworm, he was out of the tree tent in a flash.

Alec heard a brief scuffle in the leaves outside and nearby. Then, *whisk*, the otter bounded back in, carrying something small in his mouth. At the same time a tiny, shrill mind-voice began to shriek and scream.

"Bite, kill, eat, fight, bite, kill, fight, eat," it went on, over and over. Small though it was, the mind-voice exuded sheer savagery and hatred to an astonishing degree. Alec could see that Slider was holding in his iron otter's jaws a tiny, brown animal, like a small mouse, which had a sharply-pointed nose but invisible ears and eyes. The otter held the little thing delicately by the scruff of its neck, but as Alec watched, it turned around and tried to sink its tiny fangs into the larger animal's lip. Slider snarled and shook it once, then flipped it over in front of the raccoon. Scratch instantly moved one of his long-clawed front feet in a hard-smashing blow. The savage little mind-voice in Alec's brain stopped abruptly and the tiny animal lay there, limp and unconscious on the bed of brown needles.

Alec had never seen or heard of a shrew before, but the assembled animals managed to make it plain to him that these common, tiny creatures were impossible to talk to and never stopped either killing or eating except when asleep. They also fought each other and were cannibals, attacking anything they could smell or hear. There were hundreds of them in the forest, but fortunately they were solitary creatures and did not combine in groups. Whisperfoot, as a mouse, dreaded the tiny killers, for mice were a favorite prey of theirs.

"That's the whole crowd," said Slider. "That last little one and his kind are no harm to us big ones. They're too small. They get so hungry they have to eat every second they're awake, that's their trouble."

"What about the others, though, Slider?" said Alec, sending pictures of the mink and the weasel to the otter's brain. "Can't you make them see what it means to have thousands of rats coming in here? They could be a great help. Aren't they great fighters and don't they often kill rats anyway?"

"Yes, they do, but they won't do it for or with

128

anyone else," replied the otter. "Always act for themselves, that crowd. They said, when I spoke to them (and they listen when I speak) that they'd kill all the rats by themselves, when and if they came—the rats, I mean. I tried to tell them that odds of fifty to one were too much and they'd find it out later, but it made no impression. It was all we could do to get them to hunt away from the woods for a while. That was absolutely all they would agree to, and the rest of us had to get pretty rough before they would even do that. No, I'm afraid we'll have to plan without them. Too undependable, if not plain untrustworthy."

"Yes," added the skunk. "Now who else is there? Do you think Soft Wing's big cousin means it and will really help?"

"All he said was, 'Let me know the time and place,'" said the owl. "But he should come. He's reliable enough even if he makes you all nervous. As a matter of fact," he confided, "he makes *me* a little nervous, but I never heard him break his word."

"What about the foxes I saw?" said Alec. "And there was a 'possum too, wasn't there, and more skunks? And what about the deer? They could crush a lot of rats under their hooves and spear them with their horns, couldn't they?"

The animals looked at each other, rather dismayed. Things that were plain and obvious to them apparently had to be explained to this young human in detail, and yet he was now supposed to lead them.

It was the big raccoon who restored their confidence.

"Look," he said, addressing not Alec, but the animals, "there's no reason why he should know everything about life down here. After all, he only came here a few days ago. It's no discredit to him that he wasn't taught more about all of us and how we live. We need him and we have to do the teaching.

"He's already picked up quite a lot," Scratch continued, "and we just have to keep on letting him see how it goes out in the wild."

He turned back with his mind to Alec and he sensed at once that Alec had caught the feeling of doubt and distress at his ignorance and he felt that he had somehow let his friends down.

"Now, don't worry," said Scratch. "You just have to learn a lot in a short time. We should be worried, not you, because we ought to know that you can't have learned everything about us—not yet, you can't. Stamper, tell him why the deer are no good to us."

The skunk promptly took up the tale in his quiet, calming mind-voice.

"First, though, you asked about the foxes. Well, there are about six of them and they may help and they may not. Funny, twitchy, changeable folk, the red foxes. They want to know everything anyone else does and they say they'll think about it, and go off laughing to themselves. At least they aren't hunting around here, which is something, and they may end up helping. Mark them as possible, not certain.

"There are fourteen of us skunks and we'll all help. There's one family of opossums and what they'll do is beyond any of us. They really are the strangest animals in the whole forest. They can actually stop thinking thoughts, so you can't hear them at all! You can talk to one all day and never get him to admit he's even heard you. Then he'll finally say something that has nothing to do with anything you said before, and walk away. We find them a puzzle. Their minds don't seem to work like ours. More like a frog's or turtle's, really."

The skunk went on. "Finally, there's the deer. Well, forget them. I don't know why they bothered to come the other night, except to eat grass. You mentioned the sharp stickers on their heads, Watcher. Well, only the male deer have them, and they only get them in the fall. Those things are soft and tender now and no good for anything. And what do they use them for, I ask you? Fighting with each other over females, that's all.

"Their hooves are sharp and they can fight with them all right, but they only use them when they're attacked. We could probably murder the whole rat army if we had them on our side, but there won't be a chance of that."

"Silly idiots! I asked one of them to help," cut in the owl suddenly. "What do you think he said? 'Who, we deer? We can't fight. We'll just move to another wood. Ask us to mess around with a lot of grubby, little animals and get our hooves all dirty with blood? Really!' "

"Yes," said the otter in agreement. "That's the deer for you. Forget them. They can't think of anything but green leaves and running around at night jumping over things. And they think they're better than anyone else. Won't even say 'hello' if you pass one, just look the other way and pretend no one's there. They're hopeless."

"What about squirrels and chipmunks and those animals?" said Alec. He was trying to draw up a list in his mind of how many creatures he could depend on, and it didn't look very good so far.

"They are all my relatives," broke in the slow, bumbling voice of Stuffer. As usual, he had simply been sitting up and staring, pop-eyed, so that only an occasional twitch of his nose prevented his looking like a dead, stuffed animal. "Some aren't so bad. The gray squirrels are all right, but they don't like coming down on the ground, at least not to fight. They say they may come and they may not. They change their minds all the time, just like the foxes. We can't count on them. The chipmunks are too small. You can't ask them to fight brown rats. They're like Whisperfoot up there—willing to help, but no good for fighting."

He ruminated a moment, then went on. "There's a few red squirrels around, and they might fight. Goodness knows, they fight with each other enough. But they hate leaving their trees worse than the grays. They're pretty small, too. So don't plan on them. That leaves us woodchucks. There's only six of us grownups and we'll all be there when we're needed." Stuffer sat back in silence again, having nothing more to add.

Nor did anyone else. Alec was counting up in his mind. Six woodchucks, fourteen skunks, one raccoon —"Four raccoons," cut in Scratch—four raccoons, seven otters—"Four, I'm afraid," said Slider, "three are cubs"—four otters, one owl—"Don't forget my big cousin with the ears," said Soft Wing—two owls. That was it. Plus some foxes and squirrels who were fairly good chances, and some 'possums who were pretty bad ones. If the doubtful animals showed up, perhaps between thirty and fifty were available for the actual fighting line. This small number against what might amount to thousands of big, tough rats. The boy's heart sank. These were grim odds!

"What about the birds?" he asked Soft Wing. "Are you and your big cousin the only ones who will help? Aren't birds afraid of a lot of rats eating their eggs and babies?"

The barred owl ruffled his feathers and blinked several times. Even in the deep shadow of the giant fir tree, he seemed to feel there was too much light. It also appeared he was thinking hard. Finally he reached a decision on what he was brooding over.

"I'm afraid they mostly won't be any good. Most birds aren't very organized, not in the same way we are here, except for crows. And they wouldn't help anybody who had an owl on their side. They hate owls worse than anyone else. I'd drop out and leave the woods, and I could persuade my big cousin too, I think, but it wouldn't do any good.

"You see, the rats are coming at night. That's the only thing we're sure of. They can't come in daylight because even the humans would see them then. If that happened, it would be the end of them and they know it. So it means night work. Well, there's only me and cousin Death Grip for that. The other night birds are small and eat insects. They couldn't do a thing. If it were daytime fighting, we could get a few hawks, maybe even old White Head, the eagle from over east at the big river. But not at night. We two are the only birds who can do much for you."

Alec was discouraged. Wherever he turned, it seemed, a refusal of help was the answer.

"But there *is* someone else," said his own subconscious mind. He had forgotten all about the word of Manibozo. Mowheen, the black bear! Would he help? And who would find out? He tried to catch himself, suddenly realizing that if the thought of a bear frightened him, it would probably paralyze the others, the smaller animals. But he was too late.

"What's that?" Whisperfoot said quickly. "What did you have in your mind? That huge thing? What's he got to do with this? Why are you frightened?"

"I didn't want to show him to you," the boy said

miserably. "The, well, the *Person* whom I talked to when I lay down there, down in the woods, he told me that Mowheen might help us. I learned that Mowheen meant a bear. That means there's a bear around here somewhere."

"Bear!" The mouse's tone was shocked. "That giant animal? He only passes through the wood once in a great while. When he does, the forest falls silent until he is gone. I have never seen him but others have. He can break a tree with one blow. What would he do for us?"

"Yes, what are you thinking about?" demanded Scratch. "Not of asking that old terror, are you? We don't even know where he is, not now. He only comes here later in the summer. He's in a terrible temper most of the time, always mad about something."

"I don't know," said Alec. "But the great Person who spoke to me, and who made you get a human to help, said the bear might help, too. You know, I was told by my Grandpa that there were no more bears in this area. They're all supposed to be dead and killed a hundred years ago."

"So much for what *humans* know," Scratch said. "I told you, he doesn't live around here. He's supposed to live away up west, in the hills. But he comes down now and then. There's a patch of blueberries beyond the swamp that he goes to. Every one of us knows right away when he comes and we all hide."

Whisperfoot shivered. "He eats us, or anything

135

else he finds—ants, bee's nests, skunk cabbage, there's nothing he won't eat."

Alec thought for a moment. Then he said, "Look, if there's a truce going on, nobody around The Lot hunting, why wouldn't he behave? He can't want a gang of garbage rats in The Lot running things and chasing everything else out. Why shouldn't he be asked?"

The picture of what the animals all thought about the big bear was that of a great, snarling, destructive force, ranging the woods in a growling fury. He smashed bushes flat for no reason at all, and attacked any animal he saw, large or small, even when not hungry. It was a frightening picture and Alec felt goose pimples come out on his skin as he took it in.

"No, that's not what we meant, not quite," said the raccoon in a critical manner. He was like an English teacher who wants every sentence to say *exactly* what he means. "We're all afraid of him; who wouldn't be? But we're sorry for him, too. You see he's always alone. We think that's why he's in such a bad temper all the time."

"He's very old," put in Soft Wing. "Owls live a long time, but my mother told me when I was an owlet that the bear had always been alone, even when she was a young bird."

Alec began to see some of the reasons why the animals pitied the ferocious old creature. There were no other bears around, perhaps none anywhere in Connecticut, and the old brute was desperate for lack of company. He probably never had a mate or cubs or anyone to talk to about things that interest bears, thought the boy. No wonder he was bad tempered!

"Maybe we'll have to think about getting him to help. I don't know how, but the great Person I talked to said that the bear might help. We'll just have to think about it some more. I think you should all pass the word around to keep an eye out for Mowheen. If he should come around, we'd want to know about it right away."

"No fear of that," snorted the woodchuck. "As soon as that old brute appears, everyone in the forest knows at once. No one wants to be in his way when he's on the rampage."

"He leaves some of us alone," said Stamper in a somewhat smug tone. Even an angry bear would probably want nothing to do with a skunk.

"I'm all right if there's water around," said Slider. "I'd hate to meet him on land, though," he admitted frankly. "With deep water under me, I'm only afraid of humans and traps."

"Too bad we can't get the rats into deep water," said Scratch reflectively. "I can swim and dive pretty well myself. I could handle three times as many rats in the water as I could on land."

"I could handle thirty all by myself," boasted the

otter. "But what good does it do to talk about it? We might even get that whole clan of weed-eaters down in the pond to help. There must be fifteen of them at least. But who can get the brown rats to go swimming?"

Alec was interested in this exchange and forgot the problem of the bear for a moment. "What do you mean 'weedeaters?' " he asked. "Are there some more animals who might help us?"

"Yes," said Stamper. "Actually, they are relatives of Stuffer's. He can tell you about them."

The old woodchuck stirred slightly as if awakened from a doze. From his mind came a picture of a low, rounded pile of dead reeds and sticks, projecting from water, on which sat several stout, brown animals with small ears and fat, round, naked tails. "They're all for us, I guess," he said slowly. "But they won't leave the water." The woodchuck's picture now showed one of the animals eating a freshwater mussel, cracking the shell with his big square teeth. "That's the boss," said Stuffer. "Clam-Eater. He runs the whole pack of them. But I don't think they can do much."

Alec had been searching his mind for a memory of what these creatures might be. Their tails were too thin and round for beavers. Muskrats, he thought, that was it. And apparently there were quite a lot of them.

"They look pretty tough," he said to the others.

"Won't they even leave the water for one fight, if they understand how important it is?"

"No," answered Stamper bluntly, "they won't. They wouldn't even come to the meeting place last night. They say that water is where they belong, and it's too bad and they'd like to help, but they can't leave. Stuffer was pretty rude to Clam-Eater, but it didn't do any good.

The boy crouched, his chin on his hands, apparently staring at the trunk of the fir tree. Finally, after several minutes had passed, he began to talk.

"We need to know two things badly, the way I see it," Alec said, speaking slowly. "Mowheen the bear, now. When he comes back to this part of the country, someone has to talk to him, to find out if he'll help. We *have* to know that for sure."

He looked around at the animals, none of whom had anything to say, and then went on.

"Next—and this ought to come first, really, because we don't know when the bear will come back, or even if he'll ever come at all—we need a live, healthy, dump rat."

"Why?" said Slider at once. "What good is that? They're hard to catch now, I can tell you, because they don't leave the dump except in gangs—and big gangs at that."

"We need information," said Alec, "and I don't know any other way of getting it. We have to have a rat; not just any rat, either, a leader rat who knows something. If we don't get exact information, they can bury us with numbers. The only chance is to be sure what they plan to do, how they'll attack, see?"

Already a plan was beginning to take shape in the boy's mind, although he was hardly aware of it himself.

"I'll see what can be done," said Soft Wing.

Now Whisperfoot said, "What about that bear? We must get him to help us. But it won't be easy. He only comes at night, because of humans with traps and killing sticks. And I've told you twice, he doesn't *live* here, but just comes through."

"We can't wait for him to come to us. We'll have to go and look for him," Scratch decided. "But I don't know where he is right now."

"You can find out," said Whisperfoot, in a firm voice. "Send the birds out. Soft Wing can look himself when it's dark. He usually comes from away up west, so that's where to look first."

"And what if we find him?" said the raccoon irritably. "What then? Are *you* going to ask him to come down here? He loves mice—for breakfast."

"No," said the mouse calmly, "at least not alone. Watcher and I will ask him, along with one other." Alec felt a qualm pass through him.

"Who's the other?" said Scratch hollowly. "Me?"

"Stamper," said Whisperfoot, "and I'm sure *he's* not afraid." Again there was a pause while this new thought was considered.

The skunk spoke first. "I'll go," he said quietly. "Even a bear thinks twice before walking into *it*. And if he goes for Watcher, I can get in between and at least delay him."

This was a very brave speech, as the animals realized, although it was some time before Alec himself appreciated it. He was, frankly, too scared to notice. No one knows what an angry bear will do, skunk-scent or no. But the woods creatures do know that a bear can go crazy with rage in a way no other beast ever does. Bears have charged into fires and even leapt from cliffs trying to reach their enemies, seeking only to deal death and never caring for the consequences to themselves.

During this conversation, Alec felt cold to the very center of his bones. He had said nothing when Whisperfoot volunteered him for the mission of seeking out savage old Mowheen. Pride kept him from shouting "No!" But the very idea of deliberately looking for the morose monster filled him with dread. The deermouse, and the others too, could see that he was frightened and they simply waited for him to make up his mind.

"Somebody has to go see him," he said at last, "and I guess it had better be me. I'll take Whisperfoot and Stamper when and if the bear is located. But the business of catching a rat won't wait that long. I'm going into town to the dump for a prisoner tonight. Who's coming on *that* trip?"

Again there was a pause. Then Soft Wing spoke. "I can fly ahead, keep watch and maybe grab a rat who isn't looking."

"I'm going everywhere you do, Watcher," said Whisperfoot firmly, "so I'm coming."

"I just had an idea," put in Scratch suddenly. "We're fighting rats, right? Well, why not get a rat on our side? He might be the biggest help of all."

"How do you expect to do that?" said the big otter. "Do you think you can win over a rat into being like us, thinking like us? Sounds to me like you've stopped thinking yourself."

The raccoon chuckled. "But listen, Slider, we *have* a rat who thinks like us. What about Whisperfoot's large cousin, the one who collects things?"

Into Alec's mind now came a picture of a beautiful animal, a large rat, but with lustrous, brown fur, a spotlessly brushed white belly and great dark eyes. The animal was as immaculate in appearance as any cat, and no more like the dump rat he had seen than a dirty city sparrow is like a song sparrow of the wild. Although he had never seen one except in pictures before, the boy realized that he was seeing a woodrat or pack rat, famous for the habit of moving human campers' belongings and leaving sticks or pine cones in their places.

"Why haven't we tried to get him before?" said Alec. "This is the first I've heard of him."

Whisperfoot said from her branch, "Wandertail's

very shy and doesn't like being near most other animals. And he lives deep in the wood with his family and won't come out, even a little way. Or at least he wouldn't before."

"Try him again," said Alec, thinking fast in turn, "and make sure to tell him that the whole wood is depending on him. It's life or death for all of us. Take Stuffer along. He's very convincing. I want both of you to try and persuade your cousin to go into the inside of the rat hill at the dump. There's supposed to be a big cave there, and I'll bet that's where they have their headquarters."

"That's an idea, all right," said Stamper, after the animals had thought a moment. "But," continued the skunk, "animals use their noses mostly, not their eyes, you know. The dump rats would pick Whisperfoot's cousin up right away by smelling him, even in the dark."

"Get him anyway, Whisperfoot," said Alec. "I'll try to think up some way around the smell business."

Around them the dimness of the great tree was a fitting background for their various thoughts, all of which were now rather black and gloomy. The light and life of the forest outside was only shown in occasional spots of sunlit green, visible through small gaps in the mantle of dark needles and long boughs. The birds sang on in the outer world, but under the tree there was only silence and reflection, none of it very cheerful.

7

Later that same morning, after his return from the meeting in the wood, Alec lay face down under a great spreading apple tree in the orchard above the house. Although he had striven to control himself, the confident leader of earlier in the day had vanished.

The full responsibility he was shouldering, the planned meeting at some future date with the dreaded bear and the dangerous trip planned for that very night to examine the dump and spy on the rats—all these things had got him down badly. He was feeling very young and miserable as he lay with his head pillowed on his arms, trying not to let the last remnants of his courage ebb away.

He was aroused by a rasping purr and the touch of a coarse tongue licking his right ear. Sitting up abruptly and wiping dirt from his face with a grubby hand, he saw Worthless eyeing him calmly. Impulsively he reached out and gathered the big orange cat into his arms and hugged him tight. He squeezed rather hard, he was so grateful for someone to share his apprehension; but Worthless did not seem to mind and his purr grew to a loud rumble. The cat even reached up and dabbed at the boy's chin with one broad, velvet paw and then lay back in the lap Alec had made by crossing his legs.

"I wish you could talk, Worthless," he said out loud, his voice choked with the remnants of hard-fought tears. "I sure need someone to talk to. Cats are supposed to be awful smart and I sure could use someone smart right now." What he didn't realize was that he had become so accustomed to the mind speech of animals, that he was thinking, even while he actually spoke, the same thought that he had spoken aloud. He hugged the cat again, his misery and fear of the future beginning to return in fresh waves of emotion.

"Now then, don't crush me, Watcher! I'm not made of old rags," came a voice into his brain. Alec froze, his arms locked around the cat, his whole body stiff and rigid. Had he been dreaming? Was he awake now?

"Of course you're awake," said Worthless. The cat's mind-voice was rather like his purr, a sort of rumbling, growly voice, but with an up-and-down rhythm in it which rose and fell as the mind-pictures came and went, something like background music in a Western movie.

Slowly, Alec loosened his grip. He looked down at the big cat and sent out a thought.

"You can talk? Why haven't you talked to me before? Do the other animals know you can talk?"

The great yellow eyes stared at him with a hint of supercilious amusement far back in their depths. Worthless got off Alec's lap and stretched luxuriously, then sat up and looked at the boy with an unblinking stare.

"To all of your questions," said the cat, "there are several answers. I don't talk to the other animals. I listen. Most of what they say isn't interesting anyway. I was brought here as a small kitten and I couldn't talk this way until I was full grown. And I don't think all cats can talk. It's this place, I think."

"Yes," interrupted Alec, "it is. That's why *I* can talk anyway."

"I don't go into the woods much," the cat went on calmly. "No need to. I have everything I want up here. And there's something down there I don't like, that sets my fur on edge. I have been down in the forest under the trees, although not far and only at night. In fact, that's when I first heard the other animals talking and learned how to listen to them. But they never heard me. You're the first one I ever tried to talk with." He yawned widely, exposing long, ivory fangs and then began to wash his sleek, orange coat. But his mind-speech still went on.

Alec leaned back against the broad base of the old apple tree, feeling weak from reaction. He was tired from pent-up emotion. The realization that

Worthless could talk, and even seemed to know all his plans as well, was hard to take in.

"I know about the rats," Worthless continued, "and I know you've got the woods animals organized pretty well. I listen to those silly mice in the walls at night. That's why I don't try to catch them. It's more fun listening and not having them know I can hear them. That's how I learned your name, too. The other day, when you tried to talk to me up here, I wasn't sure yet. But now I think you need my help."

"Do you still listen to the others from the woods?" asked Alec. He was feeling slowly more relaxed.

"Once in a while," said Worthless. "I could probably do better if I tried harder, tried to talk to them myself, perhaps. I've never been that interested until now." He yawned again. "I know most of what you're doing, but not all. I thought about it for a long while and decided I'd better go along with you. You need more help than those stupid mice and things. It should be interesting. I like the idea of killing rats, too, lots of rats." His thoughts were suddenly very bloody and grim, and Alec winced at the pictures he received.

"Are you really going to help us?" said the boy after a pause. "We can use more fighters and you look like a good one."

"I am a good one," said the cat. "All cats are good fighters. Have you got that big stump-tailed animal from the woods to help? He's some kind of cat and should be useful." A picture of the bobcat appeared in Alec's head.

"No," said Alec regretfully. "He wouldn't help at all. He wouldn't even keep the truce."

"Too bad," said Worthless. "Cats are the best fighters of all. He would have been useful. Who cares about an army of chipmunks or rabbits? They can't fight and they're no good in this business. The bobcat could have been a lot of use to you."

Alec was getting a little annoyed. The cat's bland assumption that cats were superior beings, who need abide by no rules except their wishes, was irritating.

"Now listen," he said. "I don't care how good cats are at fighting. We have maybe thousands of rats to fight, and everybody has to obey the rules. If you want to help in the war, you obey, too. Otherwise, you can stay here and eat catfood and mind your own business."

"No cat takes orders if he doesn't want to," said Worthless, his eyes glowing. "Either he helps or he doesn't. I thought you needed help."

"We do," said Alec, "but not from somebody running around doing whatever he wants, whenever he wants. We all have to work at exactly the same time and obey orders or not at all. We can't lick all those rats by each one being the boss and doing only what he feels like."

"All right, all right, no need to be unpleasant," said Worthless more calmly. "I have a right to know what's going on, I suppose? I didn't actually say I wouldn't obey anybody's orders. Your orders, though, not from some woods animal. That's why I came to find you up here and have a quiet chat. You tell me what to do and I won't make any trouble."

"To start with," said Alec, "I want you to leave any animal around here alone. All the woods animals have a truce until this rat business is settled. You don't need to hunt anyway, with all the free food you get by just asking."

"That's no trouble," said Worthless. "I seldom hunt anyway, except to try out my claws now and again. I promise not to touch anyone but rats. That good enough? What else do you want me to do?"

"Listen," said Alec earnestly, "I have to go to the dump tonight, to try to explore and to catch a rat alive if I can. Whisperfoot's going, I guess, and we're trying to get a woodrat to come and disguise himself as one of the dump rats. Want to come along and help?"

"That sounds interesting, I must admit," said the cat, yawning widely. "What else is going on?"

"It's almost lunchtime," said Alec. "I'm going to go exploring down by the pond right after lunch. I'll take Whisperfoot, the mouse. Want to come along then, too?"

"Hardly," said the cat. "I might get all wet and dirty. I'll rest now so I'll be ready for tonight." Yawning and stretching his front legs, Worthless climbed off the boy's lap and sauntered away.

"All right, Worthless," said Alec. "I'll go get lunch. Come and see me later."

"I'll be there, ready to supply any advice needed," said the cat and disappeared around a tree.

Alec ran back down to the house feeling a thousand times better than when he had left. He had a new friend and, moreover, one who could think cleverly. He felt that the problems and the endless waiting for news were not so bad now.

Rushing into the kitchen, he seized the astonished Lou by the end of her snowy apron and danced around her, pulling at the apron edge until she was compelled to spin around in circles following his laughing face. Finally, out of breath, he dropped the apron and hugged her.

"Hi, Lou," he said, squeezing her as hard as he could. "Isn't it a great day?"

"Well," said Lou, at last having been allowed to stand still, "I can see you feel just fine. Go along with you now, boy, and play some. Get the devil out of you." With her gruff words, she tried unsuccessfully to hide her affection. He tore out of the sunlit kitchen and raced up the back stairs to his own room, to find Whisperfoot and possibly Creeper to learn the latest news.

As he ran down the long hall on the second floor toward his door, his eye took in without noticing the many pictures which hung the length of the corridor. He had looked at them all before, including the painting of a little woods scene by someone named Homer, which he had been told was very valuable. Near it hung a funny old colored map of an ancient battle in Europe called Ramillies, drawn (it said) by a Captain Mossburger, of General Dopf's dragoon regiment. He had liked the old map especially, both because of its bright colors and also because all the old-fashioned "s's" were written as "f's" so that the words looked all wrong—"Ramillief," "Moffburger" and "dragoonf." He used to say the names aloud to himself as if the letters were really "f's" and then scream with laughter. Just beyond where the old map hung on the wall was the entrance to his bedroom.

Today as he rushed past the map, it caught his eye. And suddenly the fact that it was a map and not simply a picture registered in his brain. A map, and the map of a battle at that! He came to an instant stop and stared at the faded old print. The hills, valleys and streams were clearly marked in green at intervals. Between all these things, he saw the armies, shown as narrow rectangles and square blocks of different colors, red for the Allies of long ago and blue for the French of Louis XIV.

As he looked at the map, he began to think hard. This was what he needed, a map of The Lot on which to place the various animals and the areas they would fight in. If he could do this and get everything where it belonged, then all would become much clearer. He stood, lost in thought. Could he draw

151

such a map? Aside from his efforts at school, he did very little drawing. Perhaps, though, if he asked properly, his grandfather would help him.

This last idea struck him as a piece of genius. Without going into his room at all, completely forgetting why he had come up there, in fact, he wheeled and rushed down the front stairs headed for the library. He burst into the room and found the Professor seated at his big desk, buried as usual in papers and opened books, his pen scratching on a yellow pad as he prepared a ponderous attack on some other professor's latest theory. Alec's sudden appearance, however, in no way disconcerted the old gentleman. He looked at the boy over his horn-rimmed glasses, then took them off and waited for what he had to say.

"Grandpa, can you help me draw a map of The Lot, the whole place, just like a real one? I want to have one for my room so I can look at it whenever I want and see where I've been and where everything goes and—well, like that."

All of this came out in one tremendous burst and the words ran together like machine-gun fire. It took a few seconds for the Professor to absorb it, and then he looked thoughtful. Getting up from his desk, he walked over to a tall walnut cupboard in one corner and bent down to reach for the lowest drawer.

"Come here, Alec, and give me a hand. I haven't opened this dratted thing since your grandmother died and no one else has either, from the feel of it.

But there used to be some stuff in here that just may be what you want. Ah! Easy does it."

The two of them, tugging and hauling, managed to pull the stiff old drawer open, and it disclosed a mass of papers, some spread out flat and others tightly rolled and bound with pieces of ribbon and string. Settling back on his knees, Professor March began to remove the various sheets carefully, examining them as he did so. Alec waited expectantly.

"Let's see now. Here's that set of colored prints of all the sea battles Lord Nelson fought in. I forgot I never had them framed. Your grandmother never liked them. She said they made her sea-sick.

"What's this? A set of charts of the Florida Keys. I must have planned to sail there once, I suppose." The old man kept up a running commentary, half to the boy and half to himself, as he unwrapped the papers, finding long-forgotten treasures and family mementos, occasionally chuckling as he recalled the origin of some sheet or other.

"Here's your great-great-grandfather's commission as a lieutenant in the Navy, signed by Lincoln during the Civil War. I'll keep that out. You ought to have it. Now, these should be what we want. Not bad for an old fellow to remember where he put something thirty years ago, eh?"

From the bottom of the heap, Professor March had pulled a sheaf of maps, laid flat and still uncreased. They were all identical copies and were

153

beautifully and clearly inked in black showing the whole acreage of The Lot—brook, fields, walls, and even individual trees if they were large enough.

"This what you want, boy? I had these made as presents for friends when we first bought the house. They're based on the local survey, but for fun your grandmother and I re-surveyed everything ourselves. See, here's the pond, Musquash Pond it's called. That's the Indian name for the muskrat and there are always some there. Notice all the little numbers in the water? For the heck of it, I went out in an old canoe we had then and took soundings, so you can tell exactly how deep it is in each part. A piece of silliness, but I wanted it to be as exact as possible. We mailed out a lot of them at Christmas that first year, then put 'em away and forgot about them. You'll never get a better map of The Lot than that, though, no matter who does it."

Alec asked whether he could borrow one of the copies.

"Borrow, borrow!" snorted his grandparent. "What do you mean 'borrow'? You can *have* all of them. No, wait, let me keep one. I'd forgotten how good they were. I'll have one framed. No, I'll have three framed, one for me, one for your parents and one for you. No, I'll have four, another one for John and Lou. I had them done before they came; I'll bet John's never seen one. He'll be tickled pink."

By this time, Alec's face had grown longer. How

many were left? He needed one to draw on, and not to frame and hang on a wall.

"Let's see, there's seventeen copies, minus four, leaves thirteen. Thirteen enough for your own exploring?"

"Gee, Grandpa, one's enough. Just so I can draw on it—things I find and stuff I see and want to remember. One'll do fine."

"Take the one, then, and go find out everything I missed and put it all down. And remember, don't worry if you lose it; there are twelve more whenever you want them." The old man carefully replaced all the papers and shut the drawer, keeping out four copies of the map. Standing up slowly, he dusted his hands and returned to his work, never noticing that Alec had vanished.

Upstairs in his room, stretched on the big bed, Alec went over every inch of the map with his eyes. Tracing the different places with one finger, he found in turn Bound Brook, the old orchard, the house itself and Musquash Pond deep in the wood.

Around the pond on three sides were strange little marks like this $\perp$, repeated over and over again. He studied the rest of the map and found them nowhere else. He was puzzled for a minute until he remembered John had said it was "boggy and marshy" down there. The little marks must mean swamp or wet, muddy ground. All the rest of The Lot was higher, so of course the swamp must all be down around the pond. He studied the pond again with more care. The little marks were on three sides; now what did that mean? The fourth side was the one closest to the road to town, the way to Mill Run. Alec thought hard, then looked back at the map. It must be steeper on that side, he thought.

The pond seemed to be shaped like the letter U upside-down, with the entrance of Bound Brook coming in at one arm in the U. The other arm, nearest the road, had the number 10 written on it twice. The arm lying furthest away from the road said 4 and 3. At the curve between the two arms the number was 6.

Feeling a sense of being watched, although he had heard nothing, he looked up and saw Creeper's face peeking at him out of the knothole. Then he remembered his apologies.

"Hey, Creeper," he said. "What's happening? Any news? Where's Whisperfoot? What about the rats?"

Creeper came out of the hole and swelled with self importance. "Nothing new. I'm keeping very closely in touch. All the news comes straight to me. Same old thing so far. The rats are going to move some place soon, and they're still asking questions about the roads and trails in this direction. That's all, though."

"Where's Whisperfoot?" repeated Alec.

"Dunno. She hasn't been around since I saw you this morning. Maybe out seeing the field mice. Well, I've got work to do. Be nice to find some cheese here this evening for dinner, now, wouldn't it?"

"Suppose I told you I was going down to the dump tonight?" said the boy mischievously. "And that I wanted you to come along. Would cheese still interest you as much?"

Creeper looked appalled, if a small, fat mouse can do such a thing. "Down *there?*" He seemed to choke with emotion. "That's plain crazy. The rats have guards out everywhere. Some of them are hid way away out from the dump. Why, a cockroach can't get near that place without them knowing about it. You won't get me into such a thing, no sir!"

"Okay," said Alec. "I'll have to go alone or with someone else, I guess. Don't worry. And I'll try to remember some cheese."

Downstairs Lou rang the big kitchen cowbell and Alec knew that lunch was finally ready.

He went downstairs and found the kitchen table set for three.

"Your grandpa's out to lunch today," Lou informed him.

The back door opened and John came in, mopping his face with a red bandana. He went to wash up at the kitchen sink and then seated himself.

After grace had been said and eating commenced, Alec reverted to a a subject occupying his mind to

157

the exclusion of most other things.

"John, are you busy this afternoon?"

"No more than usual," was the reply. "What you got in your mind?"

"I thought I'd like to go down and look at the pond," said Alec. "It's not hard to find, is it?"

"Don't see why not," said John. "Come and find me at one-thirty, cause I'd like to go too. But that consarned power mower broke down again and I got to try and take her apart first. I'll be ready for a jaunt around then. Dad-blasted thing ought to be sold for scrap," he added.

"Professor March offered to buy a brand new mower, Darden, and you know it," said Lou briskly. "You just love that old piece of tin and won't part with it, that's all. Don't go ablaming the tools when you could get new if so be you wanted."

"I don't get any credit for being a real, saving, tight-fisted New Englander," said John, straight-faced and helping himself to more hamburger. "Over to New Milford where I come from, we still drive our first cars, but around here the spending urge has took over from the New Deal."

Alec watched and listened to the ensuing battle with only half an eye or ear. John and Lou endlessly bickered in an affectionate way over everything under the sun, and the boy had soon realized that this was their tart Yankee way of expressing their deep love and devotion for each other.

158

"John," he said during a temporary lull in the Mill Run-New Milford conflict, "do you know all of the animals that live around here? All the different kinds, I mean?"

"Reckon I mostly do," said John thoughtfully. "Some you don't see much, of course. I seen a fisher marten last winter, though, and there ain't supposed to be any around these parts. Like a great big dark mink and climbs better'n a squirrel. Haven't seen one since I was a boy. Didn't tell a soul but Lou, though. The pelt's so valuable, some trapper might try a line in the woods. Why you asking?"

Alec hesitated, framing his next question carefully. The mention of the fisher marten had thrown him off. He made a mental note to ask Scratch if it were still around, then went on.

"Grandpa told me that deer were the only big animals around here. But he said to ask you because you know everything about the woods and he doesn't go out much. Is that right? Are deer the only really big animals?"

Darden selected a home-made doughnut from a pink china bowl in the center of the table and pushed his chair back. Eating the doughnut, he stared, not at the boy, but at his wife.

"Bible says you can't tell a lie, don't it, Lou?" he queried between bites. "The tad here asked a question needs an honest answer."

Lou knew her man and came alert at once.

"Darden, you been keeping something from me! What's down in them woods? Been nothing but deer all my lifetime and long before. You know something, though, don't you?"

"Yep," said John. "There is something else, or at least now and again there has been. Maybe dead now."

Alec's spine tingled with excitement as he waited for more. "What's there, John?" he implored.

"Bear," said John firmly, pouring himself a cup of coffee. "An old he-bear from the way he claws trees up high. Never saw him, but I been seeing his fresh tracks and claw marks, five, ten years back now, usually in summer."

"Darden," cried Lou from across the table. "You let this boy go down alone in them woods to be eat by a hungry bear? You ain't got the sense God gave a chipmunk! What are you thinking of?"

"Now, now, just take it easy," said John. "First off, the boy's in no danger. A bear that can even live in this crowded part of the country is so gun-shy, he won't stop running ten miles if he even smells a human nearby. Black bears don't bother people any-way, 'cept a she-bear with young. This is a male, woman, and he won't bother no one. The only way the boy'd be in danger is should word get out and a hundred crazy city people come tramping around with guns. We'd all have to wear red shirts to bed to keep from getting shot. That's why I never told."

His voice hardened, a rare thing for the quiet, easygoing old farmer. "And that's why I don't *want* no one told, either. Alec's more liable to get run over by a car down to New York City than he is to even *see* that bear. One old bear, maybe the last in five hundred miles of here, ain't bothering no one, and I want him let alone. He don't really live here anyway; just comes around once in a great while."

Lou sat in silence while Alec's head swam. Despite what the animals had told him, he had not really believed in the bear. But there was truly a bear, an old male bear, and he, Alec March the Watcher, had to find and talk to the animal.

"John," said Lou, her voice now gentle, "Alec won't be in danger, will he? You and me argue a lot but this is different. A bear, any bear, can be mean. Are you sure?"

"Think about it, Lou," said the man in an equally gentle voice. "Between us we hear gossip from all over this county. There's a million Boy Scouts up here every summer. There's all them tourists up at the lake to the west. And us locals. Legal hunters every fall as thick as fleas. And illegal ones all year, too, enough to keep the game wardens busy. And never one whisper, not one mention ever that there's an old bear around.

"He's an old brute, so spooky that he won't let any human get within sight even. Bears is shy any-way, much more than most critters. If he even saw

161

Alec's shirttail, he wouldn't stop running until he fell in the Connecticut River. There ain't no need to take on." He finished and stirred his coffee a little.

"All right," Lou said reluctantly. "On your head be it. I guess you know more about animals than most. Still, it does give you a turn, don't it? A real live bear after a hundred years or more." She turned to Alec. "Are you scared to go down in those woods now?"

"If John says he's harmless, I'm not afraid," he said. "Besides, he's not there very much, is he?"

"Nope," said John. "Only in summer so far as I've noticed, and only at night, if my thinking's right. Since you're tucked in your bed every night I doubt much you'll know he's around even if he does come. I figger he just roams a bit. Probably looking for a wife, though he'd know when he was well off if he thought about it some." A grin accompanied this last, which made even Lou's lips twitch.

"Enough of this chatter," exclaimed Lou, picking up the lunch things. "We'll say no more about this to anyone. Alec, if you see the bear, you just run. Now go along and play. Darden, are you going to sit around here all day cluttering up my kitchen?"

At 1:30 sharp, Alec tucked his rubbers into a back pocket in case of mud and ran to join John, whom he found out in front of the house. Together they set off through the orchard and past the vege-

162

table garden for the corner of the field where Alec had gone the night of the meeting in the forest. But of course he said nothing about this and simply followed John's tall figure as if it were all new to him.

But the boy did have his new map and a pencil with him. He showed the map to John, who was greatly impressed, and told him that he planned to add new details to it.

They entered the wood at the same break in the corner of the wall, and walked down the same narrow deer trail as Alec had before.

Eventually, moving steadily down through the sunlit wood, they came to level ground and the Council Glade, open and green in the bright sun of afternoon. It didn't look nearly so impressive now, but it was a lovely place anyway. Butterflies hovered over the short grass and birds flew back and forth across the opening from one tree to another.

"Funny place," grunted John from ahead of Alec. "Never seems to get trees or weeds right here. Looks like somebody mows the grass all the time, too. Gives you kind of a peaceful feeling when you set and rest here a minute."

Alec said nothing, but smiled to himself as he looked at the circle of flat gray stones. John would never know why the place was so peaceful!

Passing through the clearing, John led on, still taking a narrow path through the bushes and trees. The ground was beginning to squelch a bit. Alec stopped to put on the rubbers and he could smell new scents in the moist air.

They came out suddenly into the open, and Alec saw, glancing at the map, that they had left the cover of the wood at the point of land between the two arms of the pond. John had brought him to the base of this little peninsula, perhaps a hundred feet in length, and they were able to see Musquash Pond in its entirety. There seemed to have been no apparent change in the pond's shape since the Professor had drawn his map.

Tall reeds grew in clumps at the water's edge, and red-winged blackbirds, disturbed at their nests, shouted *"quonka-ree"* at the two humans. To the left, the arm of the pond was covered with the yellow blossoms of the cow lily and its broad leaves almost formed a mat over the shallower water. Dark brown cattails grew along the shore, towering above the shorter reeds. Clumps of wild flag iris blazed in blue clusters here and there. On the right, which Alec was studying carefully, the water appeared darker and deeper, as the map said it would be, and few lilies broke the smooth brown surface except near the shore. Spatterdock spread broad green leaves over the verge, however, and mixed with pickerelweed to form a green bank over the dark mud of the shore.

Red, blue and green dragonflies darted about over the water, hawking gnats and mosquitoes; but except for the annoyed blackbirds, little else moved.

Out in the open water, Alec could see large piles of dead vegetation thrusting up through the lily leaves. Before he could speak, John pointed out the same things.

"See all them musquash houses, sonny? A man could almost make a living with a trapline down here. Must be a dozen houses and maybe twice that many rats. I come down here once at night and the hull place was just one big splash and wiggle. 'Course I don't trap nor allow no one else to, but there's sure a plenty rats here. You can see why it's called Musquash Pond."

The boy again studied the water to his right. The far bank was higher than the point of land on which they stood, and sloped up to the screen of trees at a rather sharp angle.

"How far is the main road to town up there, John?" he asked.

"Maybe about two hundred yards," said John. "You can't see the pond from the road, but it's not too far. Just the trees and brush in the way is so thick. I can see you figured out where you are pretty good," he added.

Alec reminded him about his grandfather's map by holding it up and explained that he wanted to know where everything was on The Lot.

"What's on the far side of the road from here?" he asked. "Just more trees?"

"For about a little over two miles, yes," said

John. "Then you hit the edge of town and a few houses. That old dump we looked at ain't too far either, to the right of the houses a bit, maybe three miles from where we stand. Town's not so far as it looks by road, but the road swings in a curve instead of going straight in."

"Do you come down here much at night?" asked Alec.

"Not hardly at all," said John. "I used to fish a little, but I ain't even done that for some years back. Maybe we can get some stuff and try to hook a bass or pickerel some time if you like. Ought to be some fair-sized bass in here."

"Great," said Alec. "I'd like that a lot."

"I'll try and round up some gear then," said John. "Anything else you want to see?"

"No," said Alec. "That's all, thanks. I'll wait till we can go fishing to come back. Boy, these bugs sure bite." He had been slapping mosquitoes for some minutes and his thin, short-sleeved shirt was little protection.

"Come on," said John. "I forgot you weren't wearing a thick shirt like mine. Let's go back. The bugs and skeeters stay near the water." The pair went back the way they had come, and the blackbirds fell silent as they vanished into the trees.

8

It was late afternoon when Alec got back to the house. He went upstairs and headed for his room, and was not surprised to find Worthless curled up outside his door. The boy greeted him before opening it, glad to see the big cat.

"I just got here," said Worthless. "I've been talking to your little friend through the door. She seems pretty smart for a mouse, maybe too smart. Also I gather she thinks I'm a waste of time." He paraded into the room ahead of Alec and jumped onto the bed.

If he was hoping to frighten Whisperfoot, he failed, because she sat calmly watching him from her place on the headboard and never moved.

"Whisperfoot," said Alec, "here's Worthless. He may be a lot of help to us tonight and later on, so I hope we can all get along."

"I can get along with anyone," she answered, "even him. I'll wait and see just how big a help he is." The tone of her voice indicated great doubt.

167

"Splendid," rumbled the cat. "I'm sure we will become great friends, my little woods scurrier." He stared hard at the mouse with his great yellow eyes, then shifted his attention to Alec.

"Is this visit to the dump still going to take place?" he said. "Because if so, it seems interesting enough to make it worth my while going along.

"What do you say, Whisperfoot?" said Alec. "Did you get your cousin, the woodrat? How about tonight? And what other news is there?"

"Well, the news is fair, so far," said the pretty deermouse. "To take your questions in order, Stuffer and I persuaded Wandertail to at least come and meet us partway to the dump. You don't know how shy he is! If he'd heard about this cat coming, that would have been the end of it, right there. As it is, I just don't know what he'll do or how far he'll go in helping. There's not much other news. No one has seen the bear yet. The rats are still busy around the dump and a few scouts were seen not too far from the pond early this morning. That's all."

Alec reflected for a moment. He was still not entirely sure what he planned to do when he got near the dump, but the more he thought about it, the more he felt that Wandertail the woodrat was a key which might open many doors.

"What time are we going out?" said Worthless. "I may as well catch up on some sleep if it's going to be late."

168

"We won't leave until fairly late," said the boy. "Stay close enough so I can call you when I want you."

The meal that evening, eaten in the kitchen, seemed intolerably long and Alec could pay hardly any attention to what Lou and John were saying.

Upstairs later, lying fully dressed on his bed, Alec tried to be patient and wait for the complete settling down of the household. He heard Professor March come in from his day's outing and go to bed. He heard the big grandfather clock in the downstairs hall boom out ten o'clock. The faint sound of Lou and John's television finally ceased, their light went off and the house became still except for the creaks and groans of aged timbers and warped shingles. Outside his open window, the night was still and windless, only a few crickets breaking the silence with their chirps. Then the big clock struck the half hour. It was ten thirty, time to begin!

"Worthless! Whisperfoot!" his silent call went out.

"Here, Watcher," answered the mouse from the hole in the wall. "All ready?"

"I'm in the hall, waiting," came the big cat's voice. "Any time you want to move is fine."

The deermouse leapt to the headboard of the big sleigh bed and then to Alec's shoulder. As quietly as he had on the previous night, he let himself out into the hall. A touch of Worthless' tail on his bare ankle told him the cat was with them.

The three stole down the stairs through the library and out the French window in silence. Outside, under a mass of stars and the moon, Alec moved for the driveway.

"I'm going to follow the road to town," he told the other two. "There's almost no traffic at night, 'cause this road is a dead end four miles beyond our place. If I see car lights, we can get under cover." Then a thought occurred to him. "What about your cousin Wandertail?" he asked the mouse. "Will he know where to meet us?"

"I told him to meet us about half-way from the house to the dump," she said. "I can call to him, I think, if you'll tell me when we get about that far on the road. I've never been so far from The Lot myself, so I don't know the distances. But I'll have to tell him not to be scared of Worthless here, or else he'll run away as soon as he smells him."

"I'll leave him alone," said the cat, pacing along the drive. "I gave my word. Only the dump rats are prey from now on."

At the driveway's entrance, two paused and all three listened. The night was still quiet. Alec looked back at the shadowy bulk of the house far up the drive and wished for a moment that he was back in bed. Then he suppressed the thought and moved briskly off down the dark macadam road, easy to see in the moonlight. Worthless marched in front. Aside from the muted scuff of his sneakers and a few insect noises, Alec could hear nothing. The deermouse rode quietly on his shoulder.

For a mile or so this uneventful progress continued. Once or twice the sound of a car engine could be heard a long way off on some other road, but that was the only break in the quiet.

They had passed Musquash Pond on their left sometime after leaving the drive, and the croaking of a few frogs died slowly away as they went on.

Then Whisperfoot spoke suddenly. "Hadn't we better slow down, Watcher? This is quite a way from home. I ought to try to reach Wandertail."

Alec obediently stopped, and he and Worthless stepped off the road and crouched under a large oak tree.

He was conscious now that the little mouse was sending out a message. But it was not for him, or Worthless either, and thus he could hear nothing, being only aware that a sort of static was loose in the air, something like code on a radio. This was his first experience with how an animal can send a message "directionally" to only one other animal. He found it very interesting to think about and filed the knowledge away for future use.

"He's coming," the deermouse said suddenly. "I managed to reach him. He's not very far away. If we stay here, he'll come quite quickly. Then he can ride with me and we can move faster."

The three waited patiently in the shadow of the tree. A train wailed far off in the night and a whip-poorwill cried deep in the wood behind them.

"Here I am," said a new voice in Alec's mind and with that, Wandertail sat in front of them.

Even in the moonlight he was very handsome. He was almost as big as a small cat, and his glossy buff coat shone from countless brushings. He looked, in fact, rather like a version of Whisperfoot suddenly grown huge, even to the great translucent ears, very long whiskers and long tail covered with sleek fur. His voice was not unlike his appearance, being trim, neat and rather shy.

Now he sat, looking at Alec and the cat with no evidence of fear, obviously waiting to be told what came next.

"Hello," said the boy. "I'm glad you could come to meet us. This is my cat, Worthless, who'll help us. He won't harm anyone from the woods."

"I know," said the woodrat. "How do you do," he added formally. "The mouse and the woodchuck said you wanted my help. I hate to leave my territory or my family, but I guess we all have to help if we can. What am I supposed to do?"

Alec felt very nervous, but he could think of no way of softening his request, so he blurted it out.

"We want you to try to go into the rat's nest down at the dump. We thought you might be able to disguise yourself as one of them, since you're about

172

the same size and shape."

There was a pause. "I don't believe any animal thought that scheme up," said Wandertail shrewdly. He cleaned his whiskers for a moment, obviously thinking. "This won't be easy, you know. Frankly, the idea appalls me. I *am* related to those dreadful creatures and I know what they're like. They're very clever and they don't like meddling—from anyone. They also have smell and hearing just as good as mine, and that's pretty good, I can tell you. I don't see how it would be possible to pretend I'm one of them at all."

Alec slumped back against the tree. "I guess I just hoped too much. It's a lot to ask anyway, and I forgot how easy it is for any animal to smell a stranger. We'll have to think of something else."

"Wait a minute," said the big woodrat calmly. "I said I couldn't get into their place disguised as one of them. I didn't say I couldn't get in at all. I think I can, as a matter of fact, although I loathe the idea."

"How?" asked Worthless, sitting upright to see the rat better. "You just said—"

"Why, I'll go as myself," said Wandertail. He paused and Alec realized he was actually embarrassed. "I haven't told anyone this, but those dump rats know where I live, or used to. Two of them appeared one night not too long ago and asked me—well—asked me to more or less join them! I told them to get out and I haven't seen them since. I changed my house right away. Built a brand new one in case a gang of them ever came back. They wanted me to be a kind of spy for them and promised me I'd be a very important rat if I'd help them find out what they wanted to know."

"What was that?" said Alec, who was getting excited.

"I don't know," admitted Wandertail. "I got mad and chased them off before I could find out. They left, snarling threats, incidentally, which is why I moved my house."

The boy and the three animals were now sitting close together in the tree's dark shadow. It was the cat who asked the next question, and he was practically nose to nose with the woodrat. "What did you have in mind?"

"Why, accepting their offer," said Wandertail. "If I just appeared at the dump and said I'd reconsidered and changed my mind, and then demanded that I be let in, I feel pretty sure they'd make the same offer as before."

"That's all well and good," said Whisperfoot, "but suppose they don't trust you? Suppose they don't believe you at all? What then?"

"Then I'll just have to think of something else," said the woodrat. His manner was controlled, even jaunty, but he fooled no one. Even the cat had to respect his courage after hearing him talk. A horrible death might very well be his fate if the suspicious dump rats refused to believe his story.

"I think they'll let me *in*," Wandertail went on. "But in case they don't let me *out*, I'll keep sending messages to Whisperfoot here. The dump rats won't be able to understand them. If they notice anything, I'll just say I'm reassuring my family."

"You've thought of everything," said Alec in an admiring voice.

"No, *you* thought of my going in at all," rejoined the woodrat, "and after that, the rest was logical."

"Where should we stay?" said Alec. "I mean, while you're inside?"

Wandertail reflected. After a pause he said, "As close as you can get to the dump. I can talk just so far, you know. We can only do our best."

"Weren't we going to grab a dump rat as a prisoner?" said Worthless. "What about that idea now?"

But Alec was absorbed in Wandertail's plan. "We'll stay outside their sentry line or whatever it is," said the boy. "We'll try to get as close as we can without alerting any of them. Do you think you can get back to us fairly quickly?"

"I think so," said Wandertail. "That is," he added, "if they let me out at all, once I'm in!"

"Jump up on my other shoulder," said Alec, "and we'll head for the dump. Be sure to let me know when to slow down, so I don't come close to a rat sentry or get them stirred up."

With one neat pounce, the woodrat reached the

boy's sleeve and ran up it. Alec rose to his feet and, once more preceded by Worthless, moved off along the edge of the road toward town. No one spoke any further. The plans had been made and there was nothing to say.

For some two miles along the winding road, Alec, his two passengers, and the orange cat walked in silence. Twice, dirt roads opened to the side, leading to distant farms, but this was the only sign of any other human dwelling.

"Stop," said Worthless suddenly. "Can you smell anything?"

"Yes," said Whisperfoot and her cousin together. "That's it!"

Alec could detect nothing, but stood in the road, hands clenched, trying to use his nose as the other three used theirs. Then, a gentle current of night air brought a faint whiff of corruption to his nostrils, and he knew what it meant. The dump! He was smelling the garbage and filth amidst which the rats lived and schemed.

"Let us off here," said the woodrat. He and the deermouse jumped down as the boy crouched, and then darted away into the shadows ahead and to the right.

"What about you, Worthless?" said Alec.

"I hate to admit it," said the cat, "but those two are better at this sort of thing than I am. They know how to take cover out here. You know, get behind things quickly. And then they're far smaller, too. I'll stay here until they come back and tell us what's ahead. Let's get over behind this stone wall."

In a very short time, the tiny deermouse had reappeared and she perched on a jutting stone of the old wall by the road and gave them the news.

"We found their sentries, all right. But they didn't see us. The rats have the place well guarded, though, and I don't think either of you should get much nearer."

"So we might as well stay here, is that it?" said Alec.

"I think so," said Whisperfoot. "Look, here's what we planned. Wandertail will go up and try to get them to take him in, just as we planned. He'll keep sending me messages and I'll pass them on to you. I can get very close to the dump without being found out, and this way the message-sending will be easy. In fact, we think we can fix it so you'll be practically looking out of Wandertail's eyes."

"Go ahead," said Alec, as calmly as he could. "And remember, call if you need us."

"Right," said the mouse, and was gone.

The cat curled up next to Alec and lay quietly. He knew the message would not affect him and he had the patience of his race. He would wait until needed.

Alec leaned against the wall and shut his eyes. He was unsure about this new method of talking and worried about the safety of both Whisperfoot and the brave woodrat. He felt responsible for the whole plan, which now seemed reckless and crazy, and if the two were hurt, he felt he would be responsible.

The picture which came unannounced into his mind dispelled all other thoughts for the moment. He was looking at two large, brown rats, looking into their evil, black eyes! The link was working and Wandertail had approached the dump guards! What followed then came directly from the mind of the gallant woodrat, who was risking his life to get the information the animals of The Lot so desperately needed.

Alec saw the two guards approach and then Wandertail spoke to them.

"I had a visit from some of your people down in the woods the other day. I was a bit hasty and chased them away. I've changed my mind, and I came over to make a deal. Better get one of your leaders over fast to talk to me."

"You look too pretty and clean to chase any of us very far!" This from one of the guards, a dirty-looking rat with one eye gouged out.

"Shut up, you," said the other, an older, grizzled individual. "I'll watch him and see he stays here. You go get Notch-Ear and hurry up with it, too. I've heard about this fellow and maybe he's going to be useful."

The one-eyed rat looked resentful, but Alec could see that rats all obeyed orders, for he darted off toward the looming central heap of the dump.

"Don't mind him," said the older rat who had stayed with Wandertail. "He'll never get very far, he won't. He doesn't have sense enough to realize that a friend is always useful. But I do." The rat winked and nudged Wandertail. "Get me? Maybe you and me can do each other some good sometime, see. My name's Chip-Tooth, so keep it in mind for future reference."

As he finished speaking, the one-eyed guard returned. With him were several other dump rats, but only one of them attracted Alec's attention.

It was the very same rat he had seen in the vision, the one showed him by Manibozo. There was the large size, the wedge-shaped piece cut out of one ear, and the air of confident and brutal command. Surely there could be no mistake, he thought; only one rat looked like this.

The new rat wasted no time. "I'm Notch-Ear," he said. "I run things around here right now. What do you want? You gave our scouts a pretty rough reception when we sent them to see you. And now you've moved your place, too."

Alec could feel the disquiet in Wandertail's mind as this last message sank in. The dump rats were so well-informed that they knew he had just moved his home!

"Come on, come on," said Notch-Ear. "I haven't got all day. What brought you over here?"

"I want to come in with you people," said Wandertail. "I thought it over down in the woods and I decided I felt closer to you rats up here than I do to anyone over in The Lot. It seemed to me that if I got your help we could chase the foxes and weasels out of the area or at least I could get more protection. So I came to see what was wanted from me. Your scouts spoke of a deal we could make. But I don't know why you want me. Are you the big boss here?"

Notch-Ear stared hard into the woodrat's eyes for a moment, then grunted, "I'm boss enough for you, my friend. Let's leave it at that. Changed your mind, have you? Maybe and maybe not. Well, I'll think about it. You tell these two where you live now and perhaps someone will be by to see you one night soon. It may be that it isn't too late for you to join up and be smart. But that's also for the future." He turned on his heel to go and his guards turned also.

Alec felt Wandertail's sense of disaster as keenly as the woodrat did. Being simply dismissed to go home like this was no help at all. They had learned nothing and the trip was wasted time.

Suddenly though, as Alec stared at Notch-Ear's back through the woodrat's eyes, he saw the rat leader stiffen. For a full minute the big brown rat sat still, rigid and unmoving, as if struck by lightning. Then he turned and hopped back to where Wandertail and his two guardian sentries were still sitting.

"Things have changed, woodrat. It appears better after all for you to have a visit with us and get to know us better. Who knows? You *may* even get to leave. Now follow me and stay close." On this sinister note he turned again and led the way toward the central mound of the dump. His bodyguard closed in behind Wandertail, and the other two returned to their sentry posts.

As they scurried along, weaving between old car bodies, piles of smouldering rubbish, and mounds of tin cans, Notch-Ear began to address his guest over his shoulder.

"You may be trustworthy, I suppose, in your own way. But you have a lot to learn quickly about us brown rats. We operate by *orders* around here, and on the hop—none of your argle-bargle, let's-think-about-it-for-three-days stuff, like you woods people. We have discipline and that's why we're going to end up on top, my friend. If you really are one of the right sort, why perhaps you'll be included."

"On top of what?" said Wandertail, giving a good impression of dull-wittedness.

"Everything," snarled Notch-Ear. "Some fine day, even the humans will learn a lesson from us rats; but until then, your bit of woods will do us for a start. We're going to begin with that, see?"

"There are humans up in the big house on the hill," said the woodrat as he ran along by Notch-Ear's side. "What about them? Can't they interfere?"

"We can make humans mighty unhappy, even if we can't kill 'em," grinned the big rat leader, displaying yellow teeth. "We have plans for them, too, I can assure you." He dodged around a last pile of filthy rubbish and there before them was the entrance to the central hill.

Two guardian rats crouched by the door, but made no move as Notch-Ear and the others behind him passed them and entered the hole. Inside, Alec was surprised to find that he could see perfectly. Of course he was using the woodrat's wonderful night-eyes and even through Whisperfoot's relay, the picture was perfect.

Dropping rapidly downward, the passage narrowed only slightly. All the rats, Wandertail in the middle, ran along single file, following Notch-Ear as he led straight down a long slope. Other holes and passages intersected at right angles from both sides and sometimes brown rats could be seen crouched in their entrances or scuttling away on errands. Notch-Ear's party paid no attention to any of them, and every rat who saw them hastened to get out of their way.

Down, down, down went the main tunnel. Alec was seeing something no human had ever seen before—the living, breathing entity of a brown rat swarm, one of the strangest and most awful of animal societies. The boy was actually holding his breath as he lay, his own eyes shut, using those of the woodrat to pursue the incredible trip.

At last, at what must have been a point many feet underground, Notch-Ear stopped. Here was another opening, and in front of it were three more rats as big as Notch-Ear or bigger. Unlike any others seen up to now, they showed no special respect for the scarred rat chieftain and plainly were themselves of at least equal rank.

"You go in, Notch-Ear," said the middle one. "I'll come with you and the prisoner. The others stay outside."

Prisoner! Alec felt terror and knew that poor, gallant Wandertail was no better. Had he been led into a dreadful trap? But there was no time for worry.

The three rats, the new one in the lead and Notch-Ear trailing, passed through the hole. Wandertail jerked to a halt just inside and was prodded forward again by Notch-Ear shoving from behind.

Before them lay a fantastic scene. They had come to the lip of a great underground chamber. Deep as it was in the bowels of the earth below the dump, it was still large enough to hold many humans. The ceiling Alec guessed to be at least fifteen feet above the floor. And there was actual light, although of a dim, eerie, and unpleasant kind. A small oily stream of water ran across the floor of the place and some luminous insects, glowworms perhaps, were clustered thickly upon its banks and on slimy rocks rising from its surface. The result was a spectral, unclean glow.

On a low mound in the center of the chamber, not far from the stream's bank, lay five great rats. No scars marked their sleek, fat sides and their pale gray-brown fur was spotlessly clean, their naked tails white and shiny. Around them lay several heaps of white bones, remnants of past meals, gleaming in the shifting light cast by the insects. The round entrance hole through which the three had just come looked far too small for the great bulks of the five to pass through—and it was the only exit from the chamber. Even as Alec thought of this fact, a thrill of horror coursed through him. None of the five could ever leave, either by this door or any other!

For their great naked tails were knotted and tied together in an inextricable tangle, looking in some places as if the flesh had actually grown together. So fused and entwined were the five tails that it was impossible for any one of their owners to move so much as six inches before being brought to a halt by the weight of the others.

Nor was this all. As he stared at the strange group, one of them, a huge female, lifted her head and sniffed the air, squealing as she did so. But no vicious black eyes were focused on the entrance hole toward which her head was pointed. Only white, empty sockets met Alec's gaze. Aghast, the boy scanned the others, only to find a similar emptiness throughout. They were all blind! And more than blind

—blinded. For it was plain that they had not been born this way.

Their eyes were not simply the unseeing orbs which come from blindness at birth, but scarred, empty pits, still showing the marks of the ancient wounds which had deprived them of sight in their helpless youth. Hideous as they were, Alec felt pity for their maimed and earthbound state. He realized that this was all they had ever known or would ever know: the dim, great chamber buried under tons of garbage and earth and stone, black and hopeless, an eternal night, forever without real movement or air. And so he pitied the Rat Kings in their awful home, a home which was a tomb.

But not for long. They were all moving now, clumsily straining against each other, stretching toward the small hole that was their only link with the world outside. Alec felt a blast of concentrated evil from their minds, which struck him like a physical blow in the face. They were not helpless from their own point of view, he realized then. Instead, they actually gloried in their horrible state, felt great pride and strength in being pinioned and blinded and yet still acknowledged as rulers of their whole race. His pity vanished as he realized this.

Alec had no more time to puzzle over the sightless monsters. They were speaking. Notch-Ear and the guard captain crouched subserviently in front of them and held Wandertail helpless.

"So this is the creature from the wood?" It was the great blind female's mind-voice, Alec sensed.

"We have sent for you to see us and learn from us, creature," she went on, her snout waving in the gloom. "And perhaps we can learn from you. Perhaps we can even learn enough so that we will let you go. Or perhaps we will feast instead!"

There was a note of cruel gloating in her tone which chilled Alec's blood. He knew Wandertail was shaking too, but his two guardians held him immovable. The heaped white bones lent horrid meaning to the speech.

"Listen well, rat of the wood," she went on. "You see the Rat Kings who will someday rule all the world. Even now we plan a move—never mind why—upon the land of trees where you lurk. Our armies are unconquerable and our race will rule the forest whatever happens.

"But our way can be made easier. We will allow you to aid us, woodrat, and promise you and yours safety and a place in our armies as a reward. Is this not why you have come here?"

"Yes," said Wandertail. A nudge from Notch-Ear made him think. "Yes, O Great Ones, I meant," he went on. "Tell me what I must do and how I can help the glorious plans of the great Rat Kings."

"You show sense, woodrat," said the female. She apparently was the only spokesman, for the other four crouched silent and motionless.

"Go then, with our servant, Notch-Ear, and obey his orders. He will tell you what to do and how best to win our regard. Now leave us, for it is time to feast."

Then a horrible thing happened. As the three rats turned to leave by the same hole they had entered, Alec saw another large rat go past them, having entered behind them. He dragged a burden in his jaws. The rat spun around and flipped his load neatly through the air as he did so, causing it to fall directly in front of the heads of the five Kings, who waited with jaws agape and watering. It was a young cottontail rabbit, paralyzed with fright and with a broken front leg.

As the full meaning of this awful scene broke upon Alec's mind, he tried to squeeze his eyes shut even tighter and to cry out in protest at the same time. The darkness before his eyelids was some help, but he still shook with horror at the grisly vision he had been forced to watch. He knew that many animals killed for food, but the thought of helpless prey, dragged alive from the surface to the far reaches of the hideous underground chamber was almost too much for his mind to bear.

Fortunately, the woodrat's vision altered quickly, and once again Alec saw only the blackness of tunnel outside.

The return trip to the surface was swift and uninterrupted. Soon the boy saw the dump again in the moonlight and watched as Wandertail received his orders.

"You bring me news no later than tomorrow night," said Notch-Ear. "I want you to be able to tell me every path going around that pond, do you hear? And no delays either. You're working for the brown rats now, my friend, and you've just had a sample of what happens to anyone who gets in our way."

He turned to one of his attendants and said, "See he leaves at once and give orders he's to be admitted to see me at any time so that no one delays his news." He turned back to Wandertail, "You can stop signaling your wife or whoever it was. We knew you were talking all the time, but we don't care. Just be sure they keep their mouths shut. Now get moving!"

Alec almost gasped aloud at this last, for he had not realized the rats could detect a message. Thank goodness, they couldn't *read* it!

Now Wandertail was ushered out through the rat sentry lines, and at last the sight of the dump vanished from Alec's eyes. He opened his own and stretched, for his legs had gone to sleep as he sat crouched, following Wandertail's progress.

Beside him, Worthless stirred. "All over?" said the cat. "What happened anyway?"

Before the boy could answer, two small figures appeared as if by magic on the stone wall before them.

"All done *and* satisfactory, I hope," said the woodrat. He sat, neat and trying outwardly at least to be calm, nervously combing his long whiskers in the moonlight. Beside him, Whisperfoot danced with excitement.

"Wasn't he marvelous, Watcher? Did you ever see anything so brave? Or so awful as those dreadful, filthy creatures and those awful monsters that rule them?" She was bubbling with pent-up emotion and skipped back and forth, talking so fast Alec could hardly understand her.

Luckily for the future course of events, not everyone was as excited as the two rodents and the boy. Worthless had stolen away a little apart from the three, back toward the dump, and had taken a watching position in the shadow of a bush. Now he pounced suddenly and there was a shrill squeal. He stood up shaking a limp brown form before their horrified eyes.

"Looks like you brought company," he observed in sardonic tones to Wandertail. "Just as well that not everyone was so trusting, eh? A spy would have had a nice report to make, back at the dump. Let's go home before they decide to send more. Fortunately, this one was alone."

He threw the dead brown rat off into the brush and led the way back up the road, satisfaction radiating from his erect plumed tail.

9

Alec, Worthless, and the deermouse let themselves into the house after dropping Wandertail off on the way. The woodrat was already planning to brave the fortress of the dump again as he left them, but the boy told him to stay home and rest until he was sent for.

"You've done more than enough, if you don't do anything else at all," Alec told him. "I don't think you should go back there. It's far too dangerous now. We've learned pretty well what we wanted to know, and if they should get suspicious about that rat they sent after us, then it would be all over for you!"

As the boy said to Whisperfoot the following morning up in his room, "It's true, you know. We really have learned a lot."

"Like what?" she said in dubious tones. "That they were going to attack? We knew that already."

"No," he said, "the time and the place. Notch-Ear wanted to know about all the trails past Musquash Pond. That means they plan to come straight at us, not go around by some tricky method. And he wanted the news at *once*. He said so twice. They must be planning a move right away. We have very little time, which is bad, but we know it, which is good."

"What now?" she said. "Even if we have the information, what can we do with it?"

"I have some ideas," said Alec. "I always thought, or rather I hoped, that the dump rats would come near the pond. The pond could do a lot to even the odds against us—if I'm figuring right, that is. But I don't want to say any more right now, until I've thought about it. Right now we have two other jobs to think about. One isn't too important and we can leave it to Soft Wing, Scratch and the others. Maybe Wandertail can help them when he's had a rest. That's to catch a rat scout and find out what orders he's been given, where he's supposed to explore to, and what he's supposed to look for around here."

"But it's not as important any longer because of what we learned last night," Whisperfoot said. "What's the other job?"

"The bear," said Alec softly. "What do we do about the bear?"

Whisperfoot had no answer and the two sat silently staring out of the bedroom window.

The day dragged on. No new reports came in from the woods, but Creeper appeared in the afternoon to say that the house mice from in town were still on the job and that any news of the rats moving would be transmitted to The Lot as fast as it became known.

In the late afternoon, when the sun had sunk low in the west, Alec and Worthless lay under their favorite apple tree, up on the rise behind the back of the house. They had both spent a lazy day—Alec because he was genuinely tired, Worthless because as a cat, he never exerted himself unless pushed to it.

"It's this waiting that's the worst," said Alec. "If only something would be sure to happen at a certain *time*, things would be easier to take."

"That's the trouble with humans," said the cat. He was patting a leaf and pretending to himself it was a captured mouse. "Time means nothing, really, but you don't understand that. If something doesn't happen today, it will happen tomorrow. Why worry about it? Even your mice friends know that much. Speaking of which," he added, sitting up, "I thought your little deermouse was up in the room. But here she comes through the grass looking for you."

As he spoke, Whisperfoot's voice came into Alec's mind.

"Here I am," she said, popping out of a clump of grass a yard away. "I had to find you right away. Some news has arrived."

"Now what?" inquired the cat. "More trips to the dump?"

"Not for the two of us," said the deermouse. "What you do is your own business. Watcher and I have a trip to make tonight."

With the return of all his old fears and a feeling of giving way at the knees, Alec read the picture in her mind—a picture of a great, black animal lurching through the forest.

Whisperfoot went on. "One of the gray squirrels went over the hills to get some acorns from the pin oak wood. He found the bear asleep in the middle of a thicket. Says he looked dead to the world and probably wouldn't move for a while. Oh, yes, and he was bleeding a little from one foot. It had flies all over it. The squirrel sent a message to Scratch and he sent one to me through the other mice." She finished her message and no one's thoughts were broadcast.

Alec felt worse and worse. Not only was Mowheen probably in his usual state of rage, but he also had been hurt—was, in fact, a wounded bear!

"Who was going besides you two to see this beast?" asked Worthless after a long pause.

"Us two and Stamper, the skunk from down in the woods," said the boy gloomily. "We thought his gas cloud might keep the bear off if he got angry at us."

"Hmm," said the cat. "Not a very pleasant prospect, is it? However, I will go along as well. Faced with the inescapable logic and common sense of a cat, the brute will certainly see reason and behave in a calm manner." He began to wash his tail.

"More likely decide he wants to eat the fattest thing he's seen all season," said the deermouse in acid tones. "Who asked you along anyway? You'd probably get tired half way there and want to lie down."

"If you want to come, I'd like to have you, Worthless," said Alec. "That'll make four of us and maybe impress him more."

"Good," said the cat. "That's settled then. For the benefit of anyone else," he added pointedly, "I can move faster than most people think. Now, since we have a trip of some length, I shall go and rest. You will find me at the foot of the front stairs when you come down later tonight." He jumped up and marched proudly away down the hill.

Alec turned to Whisperfoot, smiling. "Well, you may think he's fat and lazy, but at least he's brave."

"I'll wait and see," said the deermouse significantly. "He's never seen a live bear yet. We'll just see what happens later on. Hadn't you better go lie down yourself?" she continued. "It will be a fairly long trip, and at night, too, when you don't see very well."

"Supper ought to be ready soon," said Alec. "Have you had anything to eat?" The deermouse, unlike Creeper, had never asked him for any food, and when he remembered to think of asking her, he felt guilty.

"I have a steady supply," she said. "Whenever I go out, I eat."

"Okay," said Alec. "By the way, does Stamper know about this yet?"

"I guess everyone in the whole wood must know. Stamper was sent a message to meet us under the fruit trees after all the light goes. He'll be there."

At this point, they heard Lou's brass cowbell from the kitchen and the boy got up and walked down the hill, leaving the mouse to wait for him in a woodpecker hole high on the trunk of the tree.

Supper seemed to Alec to drag interminably. His fear had somewhat quieted, but he now felt it intolerable to wait any longer. He chattered away at intervals to Lou and John, for his grandfather was out, having telephoned that he would stay to dinner with friends. Mostly, Alec let the two adults do the talking. His mind was on other matters. How does one approach or speak to a strange bear? Would the animal run away if he heard them coming? Alec had no illusions about his own ability to walk quietly in the woods at night.

These and similar questions kept him busy long after supper was over. He sat on the back steps in a thoughtful mood, holding his box turtle in his lap, while the placid beast lay uncomplaining and did not even withdraw into its shell. Eventually his normal bedtime arrived and he stopped staring at the glowing sky and went upstairs to take a bath at Lou's suggestion.

Once in bed with the door shut, he called to Creeper and the fat little house mouse promptly emerged from the knothole.

"Any more news come in while I was downstairs?"

"No," was the answer. "Except that skunk has sent back word that he'll be outside at full dark. That's all."

At this point, Whisperfoot appeared on the window sill, having come from the orchard by herself. She guessed how Alec must be feeling and had not wanted him to be alone.

She waited a moment and then spoke to him. "This whole thing is so scary, it hurts my head to even think about it; so I try not to. The only way to go through with something difficult, Watcher, is not to think about it. Then before you know it, it will be over. Of course, that fat cat *may* change his mind!"

It was her last thought which helped the most. The very idea of Worthless had made her picture him clinging in terror to the top of a small sapling, which bent under his very considerable weight. In the picture his orange fur was fluffed out in terror and he was emitting yowls for help.

Alec laughed aloud and the laughter helped to steady his nerves. "You'd better not let Worthless hear you talk like that," he said. "He may be fat, but he was pretty brave last night in the dump.

Anyway, I guess it's too late to back out now. As you said, it may not be fun, but it will seem better when it's over."

"That's my Watcher," she said. "Now listen, you're young still by the way your own people count you. Get some rest and try to sleep. I'll show you how mice put their young ones to sleep, and that's something I don't think many humans have heard before."

Although few people know it, some kinds of mice can sing—make a musical sound quite unlike squeaking. Whisperfoot's song was a strange little tremolo sound, high and yet not shrill, that wavered up and down and seemed to go on and on. To anyone else, it would have sounded perhaps like a tiny bird whistling softly to itself; but Alec could see the thoughts that went with the song, and they were the most important part.

Alec caught glimpses of Whisperfoot's home nest and her parents and her brothers and sisters at play in the cozy little den. At times he saw the moon at night through the forest leaves from a mouse's point of view and got a feeling of well-being from the winter scenes of play in the bright snow under cold skies. That is what the song was all about, the things that make a small animal happy, and he found them comforting.

As he listened, it grew steadily less light outside his window. Without realizing it, he heard Lou and

John come upstairs. Later still, his grandfather returned, driven by friends, and ascended to bed; but Alec did not hear him, for he was now asleep. The song had gone on a long time and had become a lullaby, sending him to sleep just as it had countless generations of baby mice.

He awoke at full dark, alert and ready for anything. Moonlight had replaced the sun, and came in a pale glow through the window. The full moon of several nights before had shrunk and was now a gibbous moon still throwing a powerful gleam across the land, aided by the stars. No breath of wind stirred the June night and all was still except for the far-off call of a mourning dove, which repeated its sad plaint over and over to the moon, *whup poo-poo-poo*. Aside from that, the night was silent, not even a cricket singing.

"Ready to go?" came Whisperfoot's voice. "It's just time now. Are you wearing the things you should to keep warm with no fur?"

Alec was dressing even as she spoke from her perch on the window ledge. He had gone to bed dressed in pajamas, and was now shedding these for his usual daytime clothes. Over the shirt he pulled a dark sweater, and he put a blue baseball cap on his head. He had no idea whether he was going one mile or five this time. The animals had tried to explain various distances to him, but their measurements are taken from one landmark to another—from this tree to that brook—and it was almost impossible for a human to figure out how much actual distance really lay in between.

He went to the window to pick the deermouse up. She ran to her place on his shoulder and the two of them looked out over the shadowed and dappled view. The apple trees were silver under the moonlight and masses of dark shadow crouched at their feet. Beyond, higher on the hill, the cedars stood like dark sentries on the slope.

"Well, I guess there's no point in hanging around," said Alec. "Looks spooky, doesn't it?"

"I think it looks nice," answered the deermouse. "But then, this is when most of us who are small get up. If we ran around in daylight all the time like you humans, the hunters would have mouse dinners. No—night is the best time of all, especially a summer night. Why, before we're through with you, you'll be up every night at the crack of dusk and then do nothing all day but sleep." She didn't believe this, of course, but simply talked to make Alec feel better.

Alec went down the front stairs and headed toward the library. The old house was as still as on the previous night, no light showing anywhere.

"Not going without me, I hope?" came Worthless' thought. As Alec opened the library door without bothering to answer, the big cat slipped past him and moved into the room first.

"I just thought of something," Alec said to Whisperfoot. "Does Stamper know about the cat coming?"

"I passed it on," said the mouse drily. "Cats mean nothing to him. You better tell your fat friend, though."

"I heard you," said Worthless. "First a mouse and then a skunk! However, I suppose it's all in a good cause." His manner conveyed tremendous disdain for the whole business.

Alec went out on the moonlit grass, the scents of night fresh in his nose. Worthless padded ahead of him and they went around the corner of the house and up past the vegetable garden to the first trees of the orchard.

"Fine night," came a pleasant voice from under the nearest of them. The handsome skunk moved out from the shadow, his black-and-white plume of a tail clearly visible, putting the cat's to shame. "I see we have a new ally. Good evening, friend."

Worthless was actually pretty nervous, for all his previous talk. He had never before spoken to any animal his own size, and being so close to one, and such a dangerous one at that, put him off. He did his best to be polite.

"Good evening to you. Seems a pretty small group to go visit a bear, doesn't it?"

"It won't get any bigger if we stand here all night," said Whisperfoot. "You lead the way, Stamper, since you know where it is. Why don't you bring up the rear, cat?" Her implication was clear, it being that Worthless would be afraid to go in front. Alec hastily interrupted before trouble started.

"That's the best way, I think, since Worthless doesn't know where we're going and I can't see or hear as well as he can. In case someone comes up behind us, Worthless can give warning."

This made such good sense that even Worthless could hardly quarrel with the idea. So the four set off westward—skunk, boy with mouse, and cat, in that order—moving silently through the foot-high grass of the upper orchard and out on to the bare slope of the hill beyond. Had anyone been watching from the back upper windows of the house, they would have been quite visible in the moonlight; but Alec had the only occupied bedroom on that side and they were unseen.

Stamper led steadily through the grass at a rate Alec could follow quite easily. Skunks are not built for high speed, being rather short in the leg, but Stamper was setting a good pace for one of his kind. Worthless padded along in their tracks, keeping up without trouble. Few thoughts were exchanged; but by this time, Alec had learned this was normal. Animals don't like to talk while moving or traveling, since they concentrate on going somewhere and on watching for danger. Talking on a journey is for emergencies.

201

At the crest of the hill, the boy looked back once at the rooftops of the old house down the slope. If he felt lonesome and afraid, he managed to keep it from the others.

Soon they came to another stone wall, in much better shape than the one further down. Strands of barbed wire were strongly staked through it at intervals and a tattered notice on one nearby pole proclaimed that hunting, fishing and trapping were forbidden. They had come to the western boundary of The Lot, and John kept the outer fence in fairly good repair.

The fence was a formidable obstacle to an adult human, but the animals and the boy slipped through a narrow gap with no trouble at all. On the far side, the pasture with its tall grass and weeds stopped abruptly. In front of them rose another gentle slope, going up to a level plateau, perhaps the debris of some ancient glacial icecap. This was covered by a heavy growth of low scrub oak trees, none higher than fifteen feet, with occasional blueberry, laurel, and juniper bushes thrusting up below. A dense and level carpet of old brown oak leaves lay underfoot, pierced by an occasional low outcropping of white quartz or iron-gray granite. No bird or insect voice broke the night stillness, only the crackle of the dry leaves underfoot as the little party entered the shadowed oak domain. The way ahead was clearly lit by the moon, for the trees kept out only a small amount of light.

The skunk paused for a second here and seemed to look about to get his bearings, sniffing loudly as he did so. Skunks don't see very well, anyway, even in good light, and Stamper was using his nose to establish his direction. Apparently satisfied, he lowered his head and led on through the leaves in his curious, humping gait.

"Have we a long way to go?" asked Alec after they had marched for some minutes. The noise they were making seemed tremendous to him, and the loud rattle of the oak leaves made him feel exposed and defenseless.

"Quite a bit," said the skunk, not halting his pace. "I wouldn't talk if I were you. I'll let you know when we're getting close. I'm heading for where he was last seen. He may have moved, but it's the best I can do."

They were heading northwest, away from The Lot, and the boy fell silent at the rebuke. His old fears had returned in full strength. He clenched his teeth hard and trudged on, trying to make as little noise as possible.

They must have gone at least two miles, weaving around the trees and large boulders and shelves of stone, before the skunk called a halt. Once, as they had crossed a little clearing near a great rounded rock, the skunk had checked and turned a sharp left. Alec had followed without thinking, unaware that the wise animal had caught a sudden harsh odor, something like cucumbers, from just ahead. Recognizing the scent of a hunting timber rattlesnake, he had detoured around the place and gone back to his original path just beyond. But of this the boy knew nothing.

When Stamper finally did come to a full stop, Alec found himself on the lip of a little hollow. At the bottom, the trees were somewhat taller and there were a few ancient, stunted willows and alders mixed with the oaks. A gleam of still water came from the middle of the depression, where an old dew pond had formed over the centuries, always renewed by the rains and staying unchanged even in dry years, preserved perhaps by the remains of some ancient peat bog at its center.

"You wait here," said the skunk. "He comes to drink here sometimes, and he was reported sleeping not too far away. I'll go look and see if I can locate him. If I do, I'll come back and get you."

Alec was glad enough to sit down as the skunk waddled away through the trees. He noticed that even in the carpet of dead leaves Stamper made almost no noise, and he marveled once again at how quiet animals can be.

Worthless came and sat down at his feet, looking around continually, with his tail fluffed up and ears cocked.

"I don't like this place," he said to the boy. "No really big trees or anything to climb on if we should be attacked. Do you hear anything?"

"The only thing anyone can hear is you breathing," said Whisperfoot from Alec's shoulder. "Maybe if you weren't so fat you'd be able to relax a little and stop frightening yourself with the noise you make!"

Alec smiled, but only to himself. He was sitting on one slope of the little hollow with his back to an old stump, looking down and across to the other side. The moon shone brightly on the ancient trees ringing the tiny pond and the water reflected silver light through gaps in the foliage. No breeze ruffled the still leaves.

Faintly and from miles away a bell began to toll in single strokes. Aside from this sound, they might have been out at sea for all the evidence of human life or habitation that existed. Alec leaned back, his dark clothes blending with the stump and his white face in shadow, as invisible as any woods creature to the eye. Even Worthless relaxed and lay down, and the three were silent, awaiting the return of their scout.

Just when Alec was beginning to feel a bit drowsy, a sound broke the stillness of the night. He sat up and so did the mouse on his shoulder and the cat at his feet, all listening hard.

There it was again, louder now. Could it be Stamper returning? All three dismissed the thought as fast as it occurred. This noise was coming from the north, not the west, and it was both heavy and regular, the sound of some great body ponderously moving through the brush and leaves with a muffled but weighty tread, careless of noise and the listening ears of the wild. Their three brains were almost paralyzed with fear. Mowheen was coming!

With each passing second, the sound grew louder and clearer as the monster approached, heralding his progress with a series of explosive snorts as he drew closer to the hollow.

The boy shrank back against the weathered stump, hardly daring to breathe. The great brute was now almost upon them and the one weapon which they possessed, the gas cloud of the skunk, was gone! Worthless drew his legs and tail in upon himself until he looked like a round ball of fur, his pupils wide with fright and his ears flattened against his skull. Every orange hair on his body stood out in alarm. Whisperfoot crouched immobile on Alec's shoulder.

Across the hollow, on the opposite rim and to the right, there was a screen of low bushes. Suddenly, out of these there emerged an awesome shape, towering up against the stars. The great bear had risen on his hind legs to see if any enemy had come to his drinking place. He stood sniffing in great gulps of air as his weak, rheumy eyes peered about in suspicion.

The utterly still and windless night did not betray the three either by scent or sound. The bear dropped to all fours and broke through the screen of bushes, lumbering down into the hollow on the way to the dew pond. They could see him clearly under the white moonlight, a great black creature with a lighter-colored muzzle, heavy in the rear quarters. He was now rumbling to himself as he approached the water, making a sound like far-off thunder.

Alec had had a lot of time to think about the meeting and this was part of what saved him, finally unlocking his frozen body from the fear that held it squeezed into silence. His brain ordered his body to move, and slowly the boy responded in spite of instincts that shrieked, "Stay quiet."

Mowheen had almost reached the water and was only half visible under the alder's leaves when the faint sound of movement upslope caught his sensitive ears. Moving at an astonishing speed for an animal his size, he spun around and faced the sound he had caught, his lips wrinkled back in a snarl and the great yellow teeth showing clearly.

Alec just barely managed to force himself to stand up. His small erect body was plain to see, even for the bear's bad eyes, and for a split-second the two faced each other under the moon, frozen in stillness.

The boy reached out for the bear with his mind and felt—amazingly—a wave of stark terror, a terrible panic bordering on madness. The great beast felt trapped and helpless, caught at close range in clear view by a human. And worse, he had been hurt recently. He was readying himself now to charge, to fight his way out or die in the attempt. Already his huge hind legs were gathering under him.

Yet, at the same instant, Alec's fear was gone! He suddenly felt immensely tall and strong, filled with power and force. It was as if somehow the bear had become no bigger than Worthless, crouching in a ball at the boy's feet, and he, Alec March, had grown into a giant, his head higher than the trees around the woodland hollow.

"Mowheen!" he called with his mind. "Mowheen, I am Watcher, and I have been sent to find you by Manibozo." Here he sent a mind picture of the great Spirit of the Wood.

"Mowheen," he went on, "you are to help me. I am not an enemy. Manibozo chose me to be the leader of the animals. I have been sent and you are called. I am not an enemy."

Over and over the boy repeated this simple message, standing still, his arms now easy at his sides, as confident as if he were reciting in class. To a human observer, the scene would have been incredible, for it looked as though Alec were defying the great brute, daring it to move against his orders. But he was soothing the grim and fearful mind opposed to his, calming the bear by mind-touch, until he could actually see the huge body begin to relax, the muscles lose their tension, the great gape of the jaws start to shut. Suspicious still, but no longer crazed with panic, the old bear settled back on his haunches, still glaring up at the small figure before him.

Finally, Alec sensed that Mowheen would never be more at ease and slowly, ever so slowly, he sat down himself. He even remembered to raise one hand and gently pat the tiny form on his shoulder, which had never left him. As he sat, the bear relaxed a little more, though still alert for danger, the big, pointed head weaving back and forth as he searched for more news by ear, nose, and eye.

"Speak to me, Mowheen," said Alec. "There's nothing to be afraid of. All the forest needs your help." He waited then for an answering thought.

When it came it was massive, slow and almost *rusty*, as if the bear had not used his mind to speak for a long, long time.

"My help? Who needs my help? What help? Why should a bear help a human? Who are you and why am I to help anyone? Humans have those shiny, noisy things that kill. One hit me yesterday in the foot. Who needs an old bear, except to kill him or drive him away? Go away, human, and I will go away and never come here again. Humans don't speak to bears. They hunt them with things that kill. This is all wrong, this should not be."

Alec was quick to take advantage of the old beast's bafflement. He saw that the bear was now no longer in a panic but simply worried, in pain, and ill at ease. So he spoke soothingly.

"No one will hurt you—no human around my place, I mean." He outlined the area of The Lot as well as he could with thought pictures. "In this place you would be safe at any time. You can always come there, summer or winter, to hide or rest. But in return, I need your help. And Manibozo sent me to you, remember that."

Again he sent the best picture he could of the Wood Spirit to the bear's mind. This time there was a long silence and the silvered muzzle of the bear swayed back and forth as his old, tired brain thought on and tried to make sense out of all the new facts he had learned. Finally he seemed to reach a decision.

"The Master of the Forest has sent you. I can see this, but I don't understand. I am only an old bear. Since my mother died, many seasons gone, I have never seen another of my kind. Maybe I am the last bear in the world. I am old. The cold hurts me more every fall and the wet of the rains goes into my bones and makes them ache. Now my foot is bleeding. But you have been sent by the Master, the great one whom we bears thought went away long ago. I don't understand, but I will think. What an old bear, the last bear, can do, I don't know. Why should I do anything?" He fell silent, and then slowly lay down, looking like some great deformed dog, his heavy head lying on his front paws and pointing at Alec as he waited.

Alec relaxed just a little more himself. He put one hand down to pat the cat which crouched at his feet; and at the touch, Worthless relaxed a little and his rough tongue touched the boy's fingers in a fleeting caress. Then Alec began.

Mowheen listened in utter silence as Alec told of the forest truce among the animals and the appeal to the great Wood Spirit. He told of his own coming to The Lot and of his meeting with the animals and his learning to speak with them. He spoke of his vision at the Council Glade, and of the rats and their dreadful kings, their menace and what it meant. He told of the plans that were being made and how the bear was needed. No one even noticed, beyond the barest acknowledgment of the fact, that at some point the skunk had returned and sat down silently next to the cat in front of Alec.

The story went on to its end as the boy explained how all of the animals had been told to look for the bear so that he, Alec, could talk to him and ask him for help. When the boy was finished, he simply came to the end and stopped, waiting to hear what Mowheen would say.

Again the old beast ruminated, his head swaying.

"So all your forest is at truce. There has been no such thing in my lifetime. All of this is new and I am old, very old. Running and hiding is all I have ever done. And now a fight with those crawling, squeaking, dirty vermin. I haven't seen one for years, but I used to kill them now and again. Not to eat, though. And so the Master sent you, Watcher, to ask for the old, wounded bear's help! The seasons turn and come again and nothing is ever new, but now this is new." He muttered on to himself and then fell silent, much as an old man will sometimes talk something over with himself, even if another person is there.

Alec waited. He was no longer even slightly afraid, just desperately sorry for the big bear. He knew now that the terrible monster he had imagined was actually a frightened, lonely, crotchety old being, who had spent so much time by himself that he had almost forgotten how to communicate.

Now that the bear was exposed to view in the strong moonlight, Alec could see that Mowheen's snout was snow-white with age; his teeth were worn and rounded with use and one of the great eye-teeth was broken. The wounded foot, the left front one, showed a scab of dried blood. Alec was wondering just how badly Mowheen was hurt, and how old he really was when the bear spoke again.

"I must think about it. Send a message to tell me when the rats come and when I am wanted. But I don't say I'll help. Tell whoever you send to wait if I'm gone." He stopped talking a minute and then slowly went on, as if a new thought had occurred to him.

"What difference will it make? Why should I

help, the last of the three—wolf, panther, and bear? I may be dying. I am so old. Why should I care?"

Mowheen turned and limped off down to the dew pond. He drank slowly and then walked off into the west without speaking again. Alec stood up and shuddered. He no longer felt strong. Now he was terribly tired, as if he had been running hard for an hour.

Stamper led the way home, as before, and Alec fell in behind him with the cat bringing up the rear. On the boy's shoulder, the deermouse rode proudly. All of the animals felt proud. None of them had flinched. In the face of terror they had stood firm.

But Alec now felt exhausted and disappointed as well. Mowheen was far older than the boy had realized. His old brain seemed incapable of retaining thoughts for long and he appeared to feel that the struggle to save The Lot was none of his business. Would he really help when the time came?

Weary and disillusioned, Alec plodded back along the track through the oak forest and over the hills, until at last the final rise was cleared and the peaceful expanse of The Lot lay spread out below.

10

It was an extremely hot afternoon, one of those summer days which seem to be always just on the verge of a storm. The blazing blue sky was full of huge white thunderheads, but little rain fell, although the noise of thunder could be heard continually muttering in the distance. A few scattered showers earlier had sprayed a little water on the grass and trees; but the roof of the house was dry again five minutes after each cloudburst had passed. A scorching wind blew in fitful gusts, each blast making the skin tingle and prickle as if electricity were somehow in the wind.

Alec sat under what had come to be his favorite apple tree, above and behind the house. It was under these branches that he had learned Worthless could talk, and the orange cat was now lying beside him.

Six days had gone by since the midnight meeting with the old bear. The intervening days had been useful to Alec, although the strain of waiting had become no easier. The courage he had shown in facing the bear alone in the night had made him more confident but also more worried. He had seen Scratch and Stuffer the following day, down in the woods, and the obvious respect shown by the big raccoon and the old woodchuck made him secretly thrill with pride. But he knew that all was not going as well as they thought. No more news of Mowheen had come in and he seemed to have vanished again. Who could say whether the ancient animal planned to help or was even capable of doing so? And ominous information had trickled in from the dump. The brown rats were very actively gathering food. And more rats were beginning to come to the dump from other parts of town as well! It didn't take Alec long to realize what this meant.

"This is it," he said to Whisperfoot when he heard the news. "They're calling in all the little groups that normally don't live in the dump itself. Then, when they do march, they'll have that many more along with them. They don't plan to leave even one rat behind. They want every single one to join their army."

Alec had asked that the mice try even harder to get more news, and they were doing their best. Beyond this, there were only a few things the boy could do, for other developments had taken place.

There had been several attempts by the woods folk to capture a live rat scout who might reveal information about the plans of the dump's rulers. But every rat captured fought to the death. There were no live prisoners. Alec wondered whether the awful Rat Kings might not have the power to compel their subjects not to be taken prisoner. It seemed possible, but the boy simply gave orders that the scouts were to be driven back and not attacked in the future. He had developed such a loathing and fear of the awful rat rulers that he was afraid continual attacks might alert them to the fact that The Lot itself was organized. Only if this fact came as a last-minute surprise could he hope to defeat the swarming rat hordes of the dump.

"Aren't you supposed to go down into the lower wood for a meeting today?" asked the cat, stretching and arching his broad back.

"I'm about to go right now," answered Alec. "Want to come along? You ought to meet the others, you know."

"I don't see why," was the answer. "I met the skunk—decent enough sort, I suppose—and the woodrat and your pet mouse. They're doing their best, I guess; but I see no need to mix further. Anyway," he added, with a flash of honesty, "I don't like it down there in the trees. The whole place is—sort of watching me all the time. At least I get that feeling. I'll stay up here until you need me to go on a dangerous trip or protect you or something."

Alec tickled Worthless until the cat rolled over with his feet in the air, purring loudly.

Alec spoke to him. "It seems to me you were going to talk to old Mowheen the other night, and argue him into being a friend. What happened?"

"I hadn't a chance!" said the cat, sitting up at once and glaring indignantly at Alec. "You took over too quickly. I was preparing a whole lot of clever things to say, in case you didn't get along too well; but then, 'Why bother,' I said to myself, 'when it's all going so smoothly?' I was ready to step in at any time. No point in shaking the tree when the birds are on the ground, as my mother used to say."

Alec laughed. "I was only teasing," he said, seizing Worthless and hugging him. "You were very brave. Even Whisperfoot said so, and she doesn't like cats too much. You know you were brave, don't you, old cat?"

"Of course I was," said Worthless, wiggling loose and starting to wash himself. "All cats are brave. Some, of course," he added, "are braver than others. I must be one of those."

"Stay here and guard the place. I'll be back by suppertime or before." Alec strode off across the orchard and fields, down into the woods, heading for what had become the accustomed meeting place, the tree where Soft Wing had his roost. As he went, he reviewed in his mind what he wanted to say. It was so important that it be said just right!

He arrived at the fir tree still brooding and the mass greeting of his friends gave him a start.

"Hello, Slider, Scratch, Wandertail," he said in reply. "Hi, Stuffer. Hi, Soft Wing. Where's Stamper?"

"Just coming upstream," the skunk's thought came to him. "I was scouting down at the south boundary. There were supposed to be some rats seen there, but it turned out to be nothing." Stamper himself emerged from a bush and trotted over to join the others.

"I left Whisperfoot up at the house, in case the mice reported anything new from town," said Alec. "Now look. I got you here because I think I finally have a plan to deal with the rats. It's the only thing I can think of, and it's taken a lot of thought, believe me! When I'm through, you have to tell me if you feel it will work, and tell me what's wrong with it. All right?"

He looked around for questions, but none of the animals said anything; so he began.

"Here's the way I've thought it out. The rats are coming straight for us, right from the dump to The Lot with no ranging out to the sides. That should put the pond pretty well in the middle of their path. My whole plan is based on that. And, of course, on the fact that they'll come at night. Now! Suppose the rats get pretty close to the woods before they meet any of us. Then suppose we start attacking them on both sides, but not in front. What would they do?"

"Probably send their best fighters out to the sides and keep the others moving on through," said

Scratch. "That's what I'd do."

"What else could they do?" said Slider. "Unless they were sure they were licked, which they wouldn't be. They'd have to do what Scratch said—go and fight on both sides where the attack came."

"Good," said Alec. "That's what I thought. My grandfather knows a lot about fighting and he told me how some of it works. The whole trick with a lot of people, in a war, is to make them go wherever *you* want, not where they want to go themselves. Now, suppose it happened like that, with some of us on the sides, and with the dump rats going on and fighting us. It would be dark, and even with all the scouting they've done, they probably don't know the land and the woods too well, right?" He was becoming really excited now and the others caught the feeling and their ears cocked as they listened to his plan. Finally, Alec was finished.

There was a long silence. The bird and the six mammals turned Alec's tactics in their minds. It was Scratch who spoke first.

"This is why we had to have a human," he said in grave tones. "None of us could have thought of this. It's going to be a lot of trouble and hard fighting, but it could just work, I think."

At this point there was an interruption. "Look what's here," said Slider, peering at the ground. "What are you doing, little one?"

Everyone stared at a fern clump beside the tree.

Out of it there poked a small, round, brown head with shiny black eyes and long whiskers. The little ears were almost hidden in dark fur. It was a meadow mouse.

"Good day," said the mouse nervously. He came out further and eyed the otter, the skunk, and the raccoon with suspicion.

"Hello," said Alec. "Were you looking for me?"

"Yes, I was. Whisperfoot sent a lot of us out to find you. Fresh news has come in, you see, and you're wanted back up there in your hole, wanted right away."

"Thanks," said the boy. "I'll see the rest of you later. So long." He ran off through the wood, leaving the animals staring after him.

Lou, looking out of the kitchen window, saw him coming out of the woods far down in the meadow and smiled at the sight of the racing boy. Alec rushed up on the porch, in the back door, and tore up the back stairs past Lou without speaking.

"Now what's got into him?" she murmured aloud. "Hard to realize how kids is either asleep or moving faster than them jet planes!"

Once in his room, Alec shut the door and sent a call. In a second, the pretty deermouse had popped out of her hole and was sitting on the pillow facing the boy. At the same time, Worthless emerged from under the bed, his eyes gleaming with excitement.

"They're coming tonight!" said Whisperfoot,

wasting no words. "Come out here, Creeper, and tell them what happened."

"Well," said the fat house mouse, emerging from the hole and jumping to the top of the bed, "it's like this. One of us, a house mouse as lives near the dump, he got pretty fresh early this morning and started poking fun at some rats who were all running around. 'Going some place?' he said. 'Lost something, like your head?' He kept it up, you know, asking if they weren't getting tired what with running around in circles, stuff like that.

"Well, he got them pretty mad and stirred up. A young one started for him, said he'd teach him to laugh at the brown rats. The mouse got ready to duck into a hole, see, when a big, old rat popped up from somewhere and told the young one to leave him be.

" 'After tonight, we won't have to bother about such little scum as him,' that's what the big one said. They must think we're pretty stupid. That mouse, he shot into his hole and passed the word right along. You won't ever get more warning than that, I don't think."

A silence fell. Here it was at long last, the news for which they had been waiting so anxiously. There was no doubt in anyone's mind what was meant by the rat's remark. Even Creeper, who was not too bright, had figured it out the minute he heard it. "After tonight." Those were the important words.

"Thanks," said Alec finally. "Thanks a lot, Creeper. Will you pass along the word that all of you have done a wonderful job, especially that mouse in the dump? We never could have made a plan without all of you helping. Honest, I really mean it."

"Think nothing of it," said Creeper, although he had assumed his proud balloon shape and looked as though he were going to burst. "Always ready to help. When in doubt, call a house mouse, that's our saying."

"We'll remember that the next time we have any doubts about anything," replied Worthless in acid tones. "Well, what now, Watcher? We talked this over and over until it's coming out of our ears. Nothing to do now but pass it on to the others and hope they'll be there when the time comes."

"What do you mean, 'hope they'll be there,' you fat good-for-nothing?" said Whisperfoot. "Let's hope *you'll* be there, and not hiding under the bed."

Before Alec could stop the row, the cat was speaking again. He actually apologized.

"Sorry, slipped my tongue, you know. I really didn't mean to cast doubts on anyone. I'm sure the whole crew will be on hand. But we'd better get moving. It will take some time to get the news around. Too bad about the bear not being here just now."

The deermouse said, "I sent out a message to him. We found a reliable bird—well, more or less reliable —an old ruffed grouse. He said he'd fly out to the bear's drinking place."

"I've never talked to any birds but Soft Wing," said Alec. "Will Mowheen be able to understand this grouse?"

"Oh, birds can talk all right," said the deermouse. "They sing and yell and chatter so much that they seldom bother to, though. When they want to, the bigger ones can get a message across."

"I guess there's not much more we can do now," said the boy. "Worthless, you and I will sneak out tonight and head for the pond. You can stay here with the house mice," he thoughtlessly added to Whisperfoot, "and we—"

"Stay here, nothing!" blazed out her answer. "I'm coming with you. After all this worry, to stay here and not know what's happening? What do you think I am, anyway?" Her long whiskers bristled and she was in a fine female temper.

"But you can't fight," said Alec in worried tones. "You're too small and it will be very dangerous."

"You can look after me. I'll be quite safe on your shoulder, I'm sure. I can duck into a pocket, if necessary." A flash of humor came from her quick mind. "If it gets really bad, the cat can save me—can't you, you fat creature?"

Worthless took her jibing in a good humor. "Certainly, my dear. I will defend you to my last claw. Not a rat will lay so much as a whisker on your tail-tip. Of course, should I become hungry during the battle

223

and feel like a small snack—" His mind picture grinned amiably.

With a squeak of alarm, Creeper fled into the knothole. But the deermouse was unperturbed.

"That settles it then. I'm coming," Whisperfoot said. "I may even be useful. You never know. Now," she went on, "it will be a long pull until we see the end of this. We all ought to rest. I'll go visit Creeper's people and have something to eat. See you at dark." She popped into the knothole. Alec suspected she wanted no more argument about going out with him and had chosen this method to get away.

"She had a good thought there about rest," said the orange tomcat. "Why don't we have a snooze until your dinner time? I've eaten already."

Alec kicked off his sneakers and climbed onto the bed and lay down. Worthless came and curled up next to him and the two were soon asleep, the long worry about the rats temporarily absent from the boy's mind. As for Worthless, no one has ever noticed a cat worry for long about anything.

11

That evening, after supper, Alec sat on the back porch and watched the heavy thunderclouds against the darkening sky. He tingled all over and felt apprehensive. This waiting was the worst part! How much longer could those rats delay? His mind roved back and forth, reviewing everything he had done or thought of doing to help his friends. The map of The Lot was propped on his drawn-up knees and he once again reviewed all the symbols and tactics.

Whisperfoot had come stealthily to him shortly after he had eaten supper. The alert had been given and all of the animals of The Lot—even those who had previously refused to help—had been notified of the coming onslaught from the dump. The scouts reported no sign of rats yet.

Now heat still radiated from the earth to the sky. The vanished sun illumined banks of cloud, towering cliffs built high into the upper air, turning them pink, orange, and gold. The faint growl and rumble of thunder echoed along the horizon.

"Sounds like Mowheen," thought Alec to himself. Just like an older general, he was growing increasingly nervous, watching the storm building and wondering what effect it would have on the movements of his forces and on those of the enemy. The boy had not previously thought of weather as a factor in a campaign, but now he sat brooding over the stormy sunset with his mind in the grip of growing nervous strain. He felt quite unsatisfied that he had done all he could.

Presently, he rose at Lou's call and went inside, where he said good night to his grandfather and then retired to his bedroom for the night, sure that he would not be able to sleep.

"Watcher! Wake up!" Whisperfoot's mind-voice came to Alec.

He snapped awake at once and leapt out of bed, reaching for his sneakers, windbreaker and cap. Outside, all light was gone. It was oppressive and still very hot. As he pulled on his shoes, Alec saw a brief flickering glow of distant heat lightning against the night sky, then the dark closed down again.

"The rain's going to come hard when it comes," said Whisperfoot. "I hope we can all get where we belong before it soaks everything. It will be hard to hear noises too, if it's raining hard. Do you think *they* might decide not to come?"

Alec snapped, "How do I know?"

Whisperfoot saw he was upset and worried and decided to say no more.

Alec finished putting on his shoes and at the same time kicked himself mentally at the mouse's last words. Rain and a storm might be advantageous to the defenders of The Lot, but he really ought to have thought more about its effect on the rats. Would they put off their move? He got up, still feeling irritable.

"Come on," he said to Whisperfoot, "let's go."

She scrambled up his arm to his shoulder and he opened the door. All was dark and quiet in the house. He carefully closed the door and headed for the front stairs.

"Use the back," came the cat's voice in his head. "The old man is in the downstairs room with all those flat things that open up." He meant the library.

Alec reversed course and went down the back stairs instead, finding Worthless waiting for him in the kitchen. They went out the back door, which was unlocked, and the three stood on the back porch looking at the dark and angry night. The hot wind moaned around the house, puffing the boy's jacket. It felt like a breath from a muggy swamp. Overhead, black clouds raced across the sky, driven before the coming storm. The on-and-off glow of lightning played around the rim of Alec's vision. The mutter of the distant thunder had now grown much louder. A first-class storm was on its way and fast.

"This is going to be terrible," said the cat. "We'll be soaked through. Who can fight when they're dripping wet?"

"We can," said Alec grimly. "If the brown rats are coming at all, they must have started by now. I don't think they'll go back, either. Come on. Let's get moving." He went around to the side of the porch and picked up his spade, left there earlier on purpose. The thought had suddenly occurred to him that afternoon that he had nothing to fight with himself. And he then had remembered John's present. Its handle was solid oak and the blade was steel. He felt that it might turn out to be a very useful tool before the end.

Bending his head against the wind, he led the way out past the vegetable garden to the lower pasture and the break in the wall. Worthless, his fur fluffed by the electricity and excitement, came behind him, his yellow eyes gleaming in the reflected lightning flashes. Whisperfoot clung with all four feet to Alec's shoulder so she would not be blown off.

Alec had no trouble finding the corner of the wall once his night sight grew better. He climbed over, followed by the cat, and headed down the narrow deer slot which led to the Council Glade, moving as fast as he could without bumping into things. In his right hand, he clutched the spade.

The wood was very dark and filled with the sounds of the rising gale. Dead leaves blew about and tree trunks creaked and groaned as they bent to the wind. The thunder was now much louder and the lightning brightened so that the tree trunks were lit with a brief orange glow. Leaves blew into his face, but Alec kept his head down and his eyes fixed on the narrow track. Once, a great crash off to the left told that some forest giant had given up the struggle and fallen to the earth, but he paid no attention and pressed on. The big cat followed steadily and uncomplainingly in the rear.

Sooner than he thought possible the lightning showed the Council Glade ahead. The tall grass at the edge of the clearing was bent flat by the wind and myriad small objects—leaves, bark and bits of soil —were blowing around and around in the air.

Alec put one hand over his eyes and plunged straight through the open area and headed for the trail on the far side. Once out of the flying dirt and leaves, it was easier to see, although darker. Still, the lightning was very bright now and the path was clearly visible in its brief flashes. The ground underfoot felt damp and oozy and the boy knew that he must be approaching the pond. He sent out a thought ahead.

"Scratch, Slider, Stuffer, where are you?"

The answering confusion of mind-voices almost gave him a headache.

"Watcher! Come straight ahead. We were afraid you wouldn't come. We're here! We're all ready!"

Everyone was talking at once.

He finally broke out through the brush at the little point between the two arms of the pond. He could see by the lightning flashes that it was crowded with a host of different animals—skunks, raccoons, foxes, and many others.

"What's the news? Where are the rats?" he asked. "Are they coming? Are they close? Don't all speak at once, it hurts my head. Scratch, you answer."

The big raccoon came near Alec's feet and sat up. "They're not too far away, over on the other side of the human road. Soft Wing and his cousin Death Grip are watching them. But they seem to be moving to our right, away from here. If they keep on, they'll hit our woods between the pond and the place where the little road from your house comes down and joins this big one."

"What are we sitting around here for, then?" groaned Alec. "We have to make them come this way or it's no good at all! Where's Slider?"

"Right here." In the next ruddy flash of lightning, Alec saw the big otter, wet and gleaming, a few feet away at the edge of the pond.

"Will the muskrats listen to you and take your orders now?"

"Yes," answered the otter. "At least they'll take what I pass on to Clam-Eater, their boss. He's out on the pond now looking around."

"All right," said Alec. "Get them all into the

water, all the otters and muskrats. Keep them hidden the best you can on this side of the pond, the side nearest the road. And don't let them move until Scratch or I say so. Even if they see the rats swimming, they still have to wait, the way we planned. Got it?"

"Right," said Slider. "Not a move until you signal. It's been explained once already to them, but I'll do it again. Good luck!" Without a splash, hardly with even a ripple, he turned and vanished into the black water.

Alec blinked at the next lightning flash and tried to see how many animals were milling around his feet. The muffled roaring of the wind and all the other storm noises served to cover the mutterings, growls, and squeaks of the animals. This was all to their advantage. But the storm-laden air with its electric effect was driving the creatures wild with excitement. Despite themselves, their mind-speech was all over Alec's brain, making it even harder to think straight.

"Has anyone seen Mowheen—the old bear, I mean?" said Alec to Scratch. An instant hush was the answer. All the animals stopped moving and it was only the roaring wind overhead which answered the boy. He stood waiting.

"No," said Wandertail. He sat at the head of a small group of fellow woodrats near the water. "No news has come in about him at all. And the squirrels never showed up, either."

Alec sighed and tried not to show his concern, but it was hard. He had counted on Mowheen.

"Well, come on, the rest of you," the boy said. "We've got to turn the rats and make them come this way. We'll have to cross the road and fight in the woods on the other side. Scratch, you lead the way. Worthless, you stay with me. Let's go."

Led by the boy, the raccoon, and the big cat, the massed defenders of The Lot plunged off the point of land and headed through the brush and trees around the eastern arm of the U-shaped pond, angling toward the road to Mill Run. It was hard going for Alec, because a thicket of thorny bushes and tall reeds grew amid the trees at the edge of the wood. The boy scraped his knees and tore his jacket in several places as he pressed through the mud and tangled roots, pushing the bushes aside with his shovel. Through the darkness and wind-tossed branches he battered his way, all the beasts following behind as closely as they could.

Just when Alec felt the bushes were never going to stop, he broke out of them and realized from the rise in ground that he was at the foot of the sloping shoulder leading up to the road.

"Come on!" he shouted, not realizing he was speaking aloud, and started climbing the slope. Over to the left, Scratch humped along, his striped tail a banner for Alec in the lightning's glow.

Just as they reached the top of the rise, a terrific crack of thunder almost deafened the boy. The rain, he guessed could only be minutes, or even seconds, away now. The lightning was almost blinding.

He stopped and took a deep breath, shaking his ringing head to clear it. There, right before them, lay the black asphalt road. Somewhere across it and to the right were the oncoming rats, and they had to be turned and headed back this way at once! Alec almost ran off down the road by himself, but realized that if he did he would get too involved to be able to give any sensible orders. By a great effort, he quieted his breathing and tried to think.

The animals had spread out all along the edge of the road and there they crouched waiting, their eyes gleaming when the lightning revealed them, their thoughts now stilled, except for formless waves of excitement. It was Whisperfoot, whom he had totally forgotten, but who still clung to his shoulder, who rescued him from his confusion.

"You were to send Scratch and his raccoons and the red foxes down the road beyond the rat army. They can run the fastest of all of us. They must go into the woods and attack the rats on the far side, the side away from us."

It was Alec's own plan and he had forgotten it himself! He gave the order, and then added, "The rest of us will stay here, right across the road in the woods. Stuffer and the woodchucks and Stamper and his gang of skunks stay in front. When the rats get opposite the pond, we'll jump them from our side, and leave the middle part open."

A mixed pack of raccoons and red foxes scurried off down the road, the speedier foxes quickly pulling away in a group. All of them, including Scratch, vanished from sight in an instant.

"Stamper, Stuffer, where are you?" Alec sent out. "Follow me into the woods across the road with the other skunks and woodchucks, then spread out in a line, not too far apart, and wait till I signal. The woodrats stay with me, too!"

The woodchucks, skunks and woodrats, all in one body, instantly flowed over the road. But looking down, Alec saw that one skunk was still waiting at his feet. It was Stamper, plucking at the boy's leg with his paw.

"Look what I have here," came the quiet voice in his mind, a hint of laughter in it. "What do I do with *them?*"

Out of the bushes had emerged a dozen low, waddling, light-gray forms, their eyes gleaming, their long, naked tails curling like pink snakes. It was the opossums, who had come after all!

"Take them with you and put them with the others," said Alec. "Can they talk to me?"

"We can talk," came a slow, grating voice in his mind. "What can we do? We hate the brown rats. They eat our food."

"Do what this skunk says," said Alec. "Come on, we have to cross the road right now!"

"Do what this skunk says," repeated the slow voice. "Do you hear, you others? Do what this skunk says. What *do* you say, skunk?" Opossums are literal-minded to a fault.

"I say, cross the road," said Stamper. "Follow me, all of you. I'll tell you more about what to do later."

Alec and Worthless were the last to run across the highway and enter the noise and murmur of the black wood ahead. They soon caught up with the others and saw Stamper put the opossums in a group at the center of the line they were building. On the left flank, furthest away from the road, were the skunks, strung out and waiting. On the right of this line, with the end animal almost at the road's edge, were Stuffer and his clan of woodchucks. Now Alec put himself in the center, with the opossums and woodrats. Stamper stayed with him and Worthless crouched at his feet, opening and shutting his claws in convulsive movements. All of them faced south and waited. Overhead, thunder roared and cracked out steadily and the lightning flickered and flashed. A gale-driven mass of forest litter was blown through the air by the gusting wind, now growing colder. Leaves, twigs, and occasionally even heavy sticks whirled through the tree trunks.

Alec crouched down beside Worthless. There was nothing more they could do now except wait. In the midst of all this noise and turbulence, he wondered how anyone could hear the rats coming, or give warning if he did hear them.

"Look up, look up!" came a voice in his mind. He did so and saw Soft Wing battling the wind just a few feet over his head, wings beating frantically as the owl fought to maintain himself in one place.

"They're coming! They're coming!" came the bird's voice. "We've managed to turn them this way! Cousin Death Grip and the foxes and raccoons are driving them. It looks like there's a million of them, though! Look sharp, I'm heading back!" His wings beat harder and he flew off to the south, back the way he had come.

"A million?" thought Alec. Soft Wing had to be exaggerating!

Stamper's voice exclaimed, "They're coming! All of you in line! Get ready!"

Now, even above the voice of the gale, the boy thought he could hear another sound, high-pitched and shrill, rising and falling. In another second he was sure—the sound of a thousand squeaking, angry voices was coming down the wind, the enraged squealing and chattering of a host of angry rats!

He rose to his feet, gripping his shovel tightly. Worthless, his teeth bared and ears flattened, stood up as they both peered through the trees.

And then they saw the enemy.

A flood of close-packed gray-brown bodies, looking

almost like water in the uncertain light, was pouring over the ground not fifty feet away and coming straight toward them. Hundreds of eyes gleamed red in the lightning's glow.

"Here they come!" screamed the boy and swung his shovel back over his shoulder. He saw Worthless gather himself and then the rats were upon them.

The line of skunks and woodchucks charged, growling and biting ferociously. The squat group of opossums scuttled at the nearest enemies, snapping with their long, sharp fangs. The little group of wood-rats fought alone, giving no ground to their hated cousins from the dump. Alec glimpsed Wandertail in one lightning flash, his teeth in a brown rat's throat.

Alec swung his shovel hard, the flat side down, smashing a big leader rat with the first blow. Worthless pounced, dropped a limp body and pounced again. Red war raged along the line. And still the mass of rats came on.

Into Alec's brain now came a wave of terrified mind pictures from the rats in front of him, as they realized that new enemies were squarely in their path.

"Stop! Look out! A human is killing us! Turn back! A terrible cat is fighting here! Skunks are killing us! A thousand strange animals are attacking here in front! A giant human is crushing us flat! Help! Send more fighters this way! We're being killed! We're being surrounded! Go back!"

Those rats who were in the front ranks were

now trying to draw back and get away from this fresh group of attackers who had suddenly appeared. But the pressure of the others behind was too strong. Those to the fore were pushed further forward still in spite of themselves, and realizing that they had to fight, they came ahead again. And brown rats are good fighters, especially when afraid. "Fighting like a cornered rat" is not just an idle phrase.

A huge rat leaped straight at Alec's face, screaming shrilly with rage and fear. Coldly, as if on a batter's plate, Alec slashed with his shovel, chopping at the rat and catching the dirty brown body in mid-air, hurling it back into the seething horde behind. At his feet the big cat was now snapping and clawing in a frenzy of rage. Stamper was not a yard away, his tough black-and-white form almost invisible. He was crunching grimly, ignoring his own wounds, tearing at rat throats and crushing rat limbs with each bite. The opossums, now far from sluggish, hissed as they clamped their long, punishing jaws on rat bodies.

Out on the flanks, the skunks, woodchucks, and other animals fought desperately, each defender faced with at least a dozen seasoned rat warriors. Some of the defenders were badly wounded and fell back, while those remaining fought harder than ever.

But the enemy still came on, their fear and determination making a silent mind-shout that assaulted the brains of the defenders. All of Alec's army had by now sustained wounds, including the boy himself, whose legs were now bleeding freely from several bites.

Down the wind from the south came a long hooting cry, echoing even over the noises of wind and storm. At the sound, the rats seemed to redouble their efforts to get forward and away from what lay behind.

"That's Death Grip, the horned owl," came Whisperfoot's voice in Alec's brain. "They're more afraid of him than anything in the world!"

And then the long-built-up storm finally broke. Thunder exploded overhead with the noise of a hundred cannons. The skies opened and a crushing downpour of rain fell onto the woodland below. The next lightning flash showed Alec only those animals less than a yard away. The rain was so intense that it blotted everything else from sight behind a silvery-gray wall of water.

The animals, both brown rats and defenders, ceased battling for a moment in response to this new shock of the elements. And that brief time was exactly what Alec needed. Raising his shovel and screaming wordlessly, he charged the cringing enemy line. All the skunks, opossums and woodchucks, soaked and drenched as they were, followed the boy. Worthless, infected by the madness of battle and needing only the example of a leader, came first in Alec's wake.

"Turn to the left, turn away from them! Go to the open side! Make for the human road, there are no enemies there!" came a clear, brutal voice which even

Alec caught. Over and over the command went out to the wet and panicked rats. It was Notch-Ear, the grim rat general. Hundreds of other rat voices took up the cry. "To the open! Turn to the road! Never mind the enemies behind us and in front, turn to the road, there's no one there!"

The frightened and confused rat horde, many of them torn and mauled and all now wet to the skin, fled from their resolute opponents and poured down to the Mill Run road. The leaders at once began streaming westward across it as they saw no signs of any other foe before them.

Before Alec's eyes the rats vanished from in front of him, so that he stood with uplifted spade and nothing left at which to strike. He was dazed for an instant and again completely forgot that everything was going according to his plan and that the next step was now in order. But one small, cool mind did not forget, and once more the tiny deermouse, clinging to his jacket, helped direct the battle.

"Follow them, follow them," came Whisperfoot's voice in the boy's brain. "It's going to work! Close in behind them. Quick, or they'll turn back! They're half of them across the road already!"

The instructions cleared the muddle from Alec's head. He wheeled and shouted aloud for Stamper, but could hardly hear his own voice through the mingled noise of thunder and rain. He remembered then that only mental speech made sense to animals anyway, and called out with his mind.

"Stamper, Stuffer! Get all your people together! Follow the rats to the road and over it! They're running! We beat them down! They're heading for the pond now, so drive them on!"

Ignoring the pain of the bites on his legs, and followed by Worthless, who was now limping, he ran through the woods in the drenching rain, over leaf-mold and sodden plants toward the road. He could hear no response to his calls but he pressed on, sure that the others would follow.

As he neared the road, he saw in a lightning flash the shapes of a raccoon and a big red fox, their tails dragging and wet, but their bodies dancing and leaping as they snapped and bit at the hindmost rats. The other, southern side of his two-pronged attack had finally caught up to him and was now fighting alongside him in the rear of the enemy. At the same time, in front of the two he could see a mass of brown-and-gray rat bodies closely bunched, some of them turning to fight, but most of them with their backs and naked tails to him, trying to get away.

On either side of Alec, more animals were coming into position. He caught a glimpse of two more foxes to his left, and a skunk ran past him almost underfoot to join in the fighting. He moved forward himself, shovel at the ready, to add his weight to the battle line. At the same time, he sent out a desperate message to the most powerful ally, and the only one not there.

"Mowheen! Mowheen! Come quick! I'm just above the road! Come and help now!"

He heard no answer and grimly attacked the nearest rats with his spade, pounding away at the scurrying bodies, yelling with the excitement of physical combat. A few of the bigger rats snapped back half-heartedly but there was no real resistance for a moment. Then out of the rain, in a particularly brilliant flash of lightning, there appeared a huge rat, one nearly as big as Worthless, with many more behind him almost the same size. The wedge of dreadful brutes came charging right toward him, actually scampering over the backs of the smaller rats who were facing the other way. It was Notch-Ear coming back to do battle with his picked troops, hardened warriors trying even now to save the rat army from destruction.

And behind Notch-Ear was something even worse! Lightning briefly showed a tangled mass of rat bodies, dozens at least, pulling and hauling something in their midst. Here was the reason for the sudden rat counterattack! The Rat Kings! Helpless now that battle was joined, blind and still hideously twined together, the loathsome rulers of the rat empire were being carried to their expected new conquest, borne on the very backs of their swarming subjects!

"There's only one human, a small one!" came the voice of the female leader in Alec's brain. "Kill him, and the others will run! Kill the human!

The huge Notch-Ear, red eyes alight and dirty teeth glistening, rushed at the boy, who braced himself for the impact.

Squealing with fury, Notch-Ear hurled himself through the air at Alec's throat. Then the boy fell, brushed aside by a vast, black shape rushing from behind him. So great was its power that Alec was spun away several feet, where he landed in a pile of wet leaves.

A gigantic paw, armed with four-inch claws, caught the big rat general in midair and smashed him into a tree trunk. Every bone in the tough, wiry body was shattered by the frightful blow. Simultaneously, the terrible, bawling roar which means killing to a bear rang out through the wood, carrying even over the noise of the rain and storm. Mowheen, last of the mighty three, had come!

Moving more like a giant cat, the great creature rushed into the brown rat army, battering them to earth with his front paws in movements so quick the eye could hardly follow them.

A combined squeal of despair and terror rose from the rats.

"Fly, run! A demon has come! A black monster is killing us all! Fly! Run for your lives! Cross the road and hide! Run, fly, escape!" The rats now fled in disorder, scuttling, scrambling and scurrying over the ground, biting and clawing those of their own kind who got in the way.

"After them, Mowheen! Go after 'em!" shouted Alec aloud over the hissing, rattling noise of the rain. He was on his feet again and charging behind the vast bulk of the raging bear.

"Come on, you foxes! Come on, raccoons and skunks! Let's chase 'em into the pond!"

Led by the great bear and Alec, the defenders of The Lot—woodchucks, raccoons, foxes, skunks, opossums, and woodrats, poured out of the forest and onto the road, snapping and harrying the fringes of the rat host. Behind them, a grim windrow of silent brown rat bodies, large and small, testified to the fury of the battle.

Across the Mill Run road, black and shiny with rain, and into the trees of the lower slope the woods animals and the boy pursued the fleeing brown rats. There was no thought of mercy in any defender's mind. The rats had come to conquer The Lot and all in it. Mindless with fear, instinctively following their fellows in front, the demoralized rat army tumbled down the slope, heading straight for the pond. There were still many thousands of them, a vast and formidable enemy.

Alec had not noticed in the press of the battle that the rain was slackening and the wind dying down. The great storm was fast passing on. Thunder was now rolling far ahead to the west and starshine was already coming through gaps torn in the thinning cloud wrack.

The boy emerged from the trees at the top of the bank overlooking the pond just in time to see the vanguard of the dump invaders reach the water's edge. Just as he had hoped, the rats, faced with a short stretch of water in front and stark terror behind, elected to swim. The leaders leaped in and began paddling across the deeper arm of the pond, their V-shaped wakes spreading out from side to side. With each second, more and more of the panic-stricken rats launched themselves into the water and struck out for the other side, swimming strongly, heads held high.

Alec waited tensely. Rats were still leaving the bank. Many were still on land, and none were really close as yet to the far side. It was not yet time. Breathing hard and leaning on his spade, he waited, while around and below him the slaughter never ceased as his four-footed allies tore into the rear ranks of the rat horde. With the simultaneous death of Notch-Ear, their war leader, and the arrival of the great bear, all discipline and controlled power in the rat host had vanished. And so they died by scores, even as they still struggled to move forward and gain the imagined safety of the water.

The starry sky was quickly shedding its clouds and the rain was completely gone. Only faint lightning on the horizon showed where the storm had passed on, that and the sodden, dripping leaves and the squelch of water underfoot. Now the main host of swimming rats was a vast oval out on the shimmering pond. The leaders were within thirty feet of the far bank.

The time had come. "Slider, Slider!" Alec's mind-message was clear. "Go get 'em! They're all in the water!"

The surface of the pond boiled in answer. The big dog otter had been as crafty a tactician as the boy himself. He had led his own family, and the muskrats as well, in a loose circle underwater until they ringed the front half of the brown rat host, cutting them off from the far bank and on both sides but remaining completely undetected in the process.

Now, at Alec's signal, the otters and muskrats struck. Coming from underneath, like sharks after helpless swimmers, they bit hard once and then went down, appearing seconds later under a new rat target.

Brown rats can swim well and even dive, but compared to otters and muskrats, they were as unevenly matched as a human skindiver would be against a sea lion. The mind-voices of the dump rats were now without any sense or sanity at all. Alec could hear a wild and confused screaming in his brain. It made no sense, being only the expression of the frenzied terror of hundreds of once-cunning minds, completely given over to the madness of fear.

The swimming rats were now milling about in circles, many trying to climb onto the floating bodies of their own comrades. It was a terrible sight and might have caused the boy to pity them. But Alec,

246

remembering the implacable menace of the Rat Kings, simply felt a grim satisfaction as he watched the fury out on the star-shot water.

All of the brown rats on the near bank had now succumbed. Some of the raccoons had entered the water and were snapping and diving at the tails of the last rat swimmers, still struggling to reach the distant, unattainable shore.

As the boy somberly watched the end of the battle, a great shape loomed in front of him. Alec saw the old bear standing against the bank before him looking up with faintly gleaming eyes.

"Was I in time?" came the message from the old, tired mind.

Alec reached one hand down to pat the silvery muzzle. "You were in time, Mowheen," he said. "We finished the whole crowd of them. And we couldn't have done it without you."

"Good, good," said the big beast. "The old bear was some use after all. The Rat Kings are dead, you know. I saw to it. Never even got a bite from the filthy vermin. You did, though," he said, eyeing the boy's legs, which were covered with blood, now mostly dried. "Better go rest and lick your wounds, little human."

His long tongue shot out and touched Alec's knee. "We will not meet again, Watcher, not again. I am going for a long walk. The old bear will go far up into the hills of the west and north. I don't think he'll come down again. Too many aches, too many seasons. This is the last. Good-bye, Watcher. Remember the old bear who came when he was needed."

The great black shape swung off down the shore and vanished into the darkness of an alder thicket. Alec felt tears come to his eyes. He suddenly felt more tired than ever before in his life.

Then a thought touched his mind and he realized that Whisperfoot was still on his shoulder. Through all the battle and the chase, the storm and the rain, the deermouse had been steadfast. Now she was sitting up, dressing her wet fur and cleaning her whiskers with her tiny front paws.

"Well, that was a thoroughly messy business," her thought came briskly. "Look out at the pond, Watcher. Nothing left!"

The deermouse was right. As Alec looked, he could see the war was indeed over. The first light of midsummer dawn showed the ripples of swimming muskrats and otters, but of the brown rats there was not a living one. All had died, many by tooth and claw, many by drowning, and some from fear alone. Of the great army which had set out from the Mill Run dump, not one remained. The menace to The Lot and its creatures was ended.

12

The boy sat down where he was, on the wet, cold slope overlooking the pond. Unconsciously, his hand went out to the head of the big cat, still engaged in cleaning his wounds, and patted it gently. Worthless looked up, his yellow eyes glowing.

"What do we do now?" came his voice. "This seems to be settled once and for all."

"I don't know," said Alec. "I feel so tired I don't think I can stand up. It seems hard to believe it's all over."

"Look at the pond shallows if you don't believe it," came another voice. Scratch appeared and sat up a few feet away looking at Alec calmly. The raccoon was covered with bleeding cuts and pieces of fur seemed to have been pulled out of his bedraggled ring-tail in clumps. Nevertheless, he seemed pleased with himself.

The boy peered at the water's edge and saw brown shapes, motionless as floating leaves. But they were not leaves.

A branch overhead shook suddenly as a weight, or rather two weights, descended on it. Water fell on Alec's head and neck as he looked up.

"Here we are, wet but content," said Soft Wing cheerfully. "Look who I brought with me! We had to go hide in a thick spruce when the rain started, but we had fun before that, didn't we, cousin?"

Next to him sat Death Grip, and looking for the first time at the great horned owl, Alec could see why the forest animals were terrified of him. Even with sodden feathers, he was twice Soft Wing's size, with huge, pointed feather ears and great, unblinking, golden eyes. These were now fixed on the boy.

"So this is the one who thought up the whole idea? Hardly more than an owlet, too! Well done, Watcher. A good plan and good sport, the best I have ever had, and I was hatched many seasons ago."

His mind voice was velvety like Soft Wing's but even deeper and with a note of menace running through it.

Alec roused himself and tried to thank the two big birds. They really had done invaluable work, and he now told them so.

"No thanks needed," said the horned owl. "There was a command, wasn't there? All did what they could, not so? Now it is over, and we can go back to our own lives again. Come, cousin, I want to fly and dry my feathers. Farewell, Watcher."

Soundlessly, the two lifted from the branch and

flew off across the pond. As they entered the darkness of the far woods, Alec heard one long "who-who-o-o-o!"

Looking down again, the boy saw that Scratch had been joined by the black-and-white shape of Stamper. With a slither and a flop, the shining wet form of Slider, the big otter, came up the bank and plumped down beside the two. All three stared up at Alec, as if waiting for more orders.

"You all did very well," he said slowly. It seemed such an effort to get his thoughts organized!

"Slider," he said to the big dog otter, "You were marvelous. It looks like not a single rat got away. But the pond is a mess."

"Leave that to us," said Slider. "Us and the muskrats. We'll stuff 'em all into the marsh over at the far end. There's a patch of quick-mud there you could shove a young mountain into. Look—out on the pond. They've started already."

Alec could see dim activity in the weed-grown shallows. Rat bodies, sometimes two at a time, were being towed away up the pond in a steady stream. The cleaning-up process was regular and orderly, otters and muskrats pulling and hauling the floating brown rats out of the reeds and moving them off to the north end of the water.

"Then I guess that's the end of it," the boy said. "I suppose I'd better get back before I'm missed. I've got to get these cuts fixed up, too." He slowly stood up, feeling stiff and sore all over.

The animals looked at each other, each one reluctant to speak. Old Stuffer now came waddling up.

"All done and not a one left," he said. "Now we can all go back to the Council Glade and settle this business once and for all." The old woodchuck's normally slow speech was almost lively for once, and although he had as many wounds as any other animal, he actually looked chipper.

"What do you mean?" said the boy. "I thought everything was already settled. What else is left?

"The glade, the clearing in the woods where you talked to—whoever you talked to," Stamper explained. "We all have to go there now. Don't you *want* to? We do."

"I don't know what you mean," said Alec. His senses were so dull by now that he scarcely knew what was happening. "I just want to go home and to bed. Why do we have to go somewhere?"

"Well, we do have to," said Scratch. The raccoon paused and then went on. "We just *know* we have to, that's all. I think you should come, too."

"I don't want to go," said Worthless, sitting up, his fur erect and bristling.

"We can't make you go," came from Slider. The big otter came closer to Alec and looked up at him almost imploringly.

"Watcher, we just know we have to go to the Council Glade right now. Everybody. Even the muskrats are coming and my people. And everyone thinks you should come, too. It won't take long. Everyone who fought the rats should go. We know this. Won't you come and bring the cat?"

Alec stood leaning on his trusty spade, his head bowed from utter weariness. The light of the approaching dawn shone in his eyes and a gentle breeze, coming from the forest across the water, chilled through his wet clothes.

"Watcher, you should come," came Whisperfoot's dainty voice in his mind. "I wouldn't ask if it weren't important."

"All right," said Alec. "I don't know why, but if you all say so, I'll come. So will Worthless. Come on, old cat. If I'm going, you have to."

"I don't like this at all," grumbled Worthless. "I can feel something coming from there I don't like, something strange. It makes me nervous to think about it."

Now that Alec had made up his mind, he wanted no argument. "I said we're going. Now come on, before we're too stiff to even move at all."

He started off slowly around the edge of the pond and Worthless, still muttering to himself, got up and limped along behind. After him came the others and as they moved, a steady procession of animals joined them.

Otters emerged from the water, and squat muskrats left their task of towing to follow them. The foxes added themselves to the group, and the wood-chucks and skunks trotted along. The clump of hissing, waddling opossums joined in, and Wander-tail led his little band of woodrats proudly at one side.

They soon saw the little clearing before them. Alec walked out into the middle of the glade. He no longer had that strange compulsion to do some-thing, but he did feel the old sense of calm and rest-fulness. Without even consciously thinking, he walked to the circle of flat stones and sat down in its center on the damp, cropped turf. Worthless followed and despite his earlier fears and his dislike of wet grass, lay down next to Alec.

Hardly making a sound, all of the woods people came into the clearing and made a circle around the boy, but remaining outside the stones. Scratch, Stuf-fer, Stamper, Slider, and Wandertail arranged them-selves in a row before him. He felt the wave of affection from their minds touch his.

"Good-bye, Watcher," came Whisperfoot's voice from his shoulder. He watched, detached, almost without thought, as the deermouse ran down his arm and pattered over to join the five in front of him.

"Good-bye, Watcher!" the other animals said. And there came another Voice, too: *Good-bye.*

A deep sense of contentment filled Alec's mind, and suddenly his wounds ceased to hurt.

Epilogue

Alec blinked down at Worthless. He was sitting in the clearing and the dawn sunlight was shining on the close-clipped grass.

"I must have dozed a bit," he thought. A muffled purr from next to his knee told him that Worthless also was asleep. He stared down at the big cat, noting that his fur was both bedraggled and torn. "You've been fighting, cat," he said aloud. "I wonder where?"

It seemed to be getting brighter fast, the morning light pouring down through the trees. Alec scratched his head and then poked Worthless, who woke up and meowed indignantly.

"We must have really stayed out late, Worthless," said the boy. "Let's get home fast!"

He stood up and felt the memory of pain in his legs as he did so. His mind tried desperately to summon up a recollection. Rats, was it . . . or was it raccoons? He almost had it for a second.

But He whose gate lay still under the glow of dawn was yet the master. A mighty will, gentle but

255

inexorable, beat down the boy's defenses, smoothing his memory, wiping it clean of all save a desire to be gone. The strange thoughts vanished.

"Come on, cat," he said. "It must be around five-thirty. If we hurry, we can get back before Lou finds I've been out all night. Let's go."

Stealing in through the library and racing silently up the stair, Alec was in his room with the door shut only minutes before Lou and John passed by on their way to the kitchen. The narrowness of the escape drove the last vestige of his adventures from his mind.

As he undressed and lay down on his bed, he heard the call of a mourning dove, echoing from the distant recesses of the wood. For just an instant, he felt as if the bird's soft call were saying, "Well done." Then sleep came and his return to his own life was complete. The strife was ended, the war was truly won, and the magic of the forest was gone as if it had never been.

Again the distant bird called and the trees and their branches, sighing in a soft breeze, spoke gently together under the morning sun.

Sterling E. Lanier

Making bronze, silver and gold figures is Sterling E. Lanier's profession, but it began as a hobby only ten years ago. That hobby has also deepened his interest in writing. Now, Mr. Lanier says, "Almost all of my ideas for books and stories come while sculpting. I have done many characters from *The War for the Lot* and am writing a second book based on other pieces. In fact, I'm three books ahead on characters."

The author, a former trade book editor, lives with his wife, Martha, and two small children in Sarasota, Florida. He has written short stories and magazine articles, but this is his first book for children.

DATE DUE

MAY 1 8 '73	MY 1 2 '93		
H 3	DEC 07 1994		
JUL 3 '73			
H 3			
JUL 1 8 '73			
E H			
FEB 2 0 '79			
FEB 8 '79			
AUG 3 '82			
AUG 3 '82			
AUG 5 1982			
JUN 1 7 '86			
JUN 1 6 '86			
NOV 1 1 '86			
NOV 20 '86			
FEB 1 7 '87			
FEB 1 6 '87			
MAY 2 3 '92			
GAYLORD			PRINTED IN U.S.A.